"Clever, playful, and gripping. A real treat for bookworms."
**Lucy Strange, award-winning author of *The Secret of Nightingale Wood*,
Our Castle by the Sea, and *The Ghost of Gosswater***

"Julia Golding's Jane Austen Investigates offers a gripping detective story with an abundance of Easter eggs for Austen fans. Golding gives us a feisty young Jane, who, unfazed by the snobbery she faces, stands up not only for herself but for those on the margins of her late 18th-century world. This is a delightful riff on the wit and irony of Austen's works; of her wonderful juvenilia, especially."
**David Taylor, Associate Professor, Faculty of English,
University of Oxford**

JANE AUSTEN INVESTIGATES

The Abbey Mystery

Julia Golding

LION FICTION

Published by

Lion Hudson Limited

Wilkinson House, Jordan Hill Business Park,
Banbury Road, Oxford OX2 8DR, England
www.lionhudson.com

ISBN 978 1 78264 334 0
e-ISBN 978 1 78264 335 7

First edition 2021

A catalogue record for this book is available from the British Library

Printed and bound in the UK, January 2021, LH57

Editor's Note

Notebooks containing details of Jane Austen's first investigations were
recently found hidden in a trunk stored in the attics of Jane's family home.
There are signs that Jane expected her papers to be discovered,
for they begin with a warning from young Jane herself.

Warning

*Any resemblance to persons living or dead in these case notes
is entirely intentional. Names of people and places have been
changed to protect the wicked – but you know who you are!*

J.A.

Chapter 1

1789

It had to be acknowledged that the life of a clergyman's daughter in deepest rural Hampshire was disappointingly full of duties. There were few things for an adventurous girl to do. That was why Jane always considered it fortunate to be in the carriage accident. Without that disaster, she would never have met the Abbey ghost.

Jane had not begun the day intending to be thrown from a coach – nor to go ghost-hunting. She had been striding along the Steventon Road behind her older sister, boots making a satisfying stomp on the ground. Cassandra swung her basket, knocking off the tops from the cow parsley. After calling on an elderly lady with a hacking cough FOR TWO HOURS, both Cassandra and Jane had to misbehave. There was nothing more annoying than a persistent cough – especially in someone else.

If only something exciting would happen! If it didn't come soon, Jane felt she might EXPLODE with frustration. Maybe she should disguise herself as a sailor and go on a voyage like those of Captain Cook – without his grisly end?

"Listening to Old Mrs Taylor is like being in the path of stampeding cattle," said Cassandra.

Jane plucked a fat blade of grass, held it between her thumbs, and hooted rudely.

"Imagine being that old! Fifty-six!" continued Cassandra.

Jane didn't feel she need add anything. Her older sister was well able to chatter away for both of them. Words were Jane's greatest treasure and she spent hers carefully.

"Did you hear what her son called us?" asked Cassandra.

"Interfering halfwits," Jane replied. She thought for a moment. "Interfering I accept, but I've a whole wit at least."

Cassandra walked backward a few steps. "What about me, Jane? Your older, more beautiful, more talented – and far more modest sister?"

Jane wrinkled her nose. "I'll allow you a whole wit, but sadly it's a dim one."

Cassandra chuckled. "I'm the dimwit?" She loved it when Jane insulted her – their family was unique in that way, liking nothing better than a joke at their own expense.

The rhythmic thud of hooves alerted the sisters to the approach of a carriage. The lane was narrow and windy, so they climbed the bank. A four-wheeler appeared around the bend, paintwork in green and yellow, brass lamps gleaming. All told, a flash vehicle for a fashionable gentleman.

Jane's heart sank.

As soon as Cassandra saw who was driving, her cheeks went pink and she rearranged the basket carefully on her arm so that no hint of her as Batterer of Blooms remained.

"It's George Watson!" whispered Cassandra.

"I know," said Jane. She had suffered all summer from her sister's adoration for the local squire's son. Her sister had rarely liked a stupider fellow.

George heaved on the horses' reins in a move that must have hurt their poor mouths and drew the carriage to a juddering stop. He gave a flourish of his hat. "Ladies!" He then giggled.

George Watson was officially HOPELESS.

"Mr Watson," said Cassandra in a breathy tone unlike her usual. At sixteen, she was in that delicate area between girl and lady. George had won her heart by treating her as grown-up.

"Miss Austen, Miss Jane, would you care for a ride in my new phaeton? I've taken delivery only this morning."

"Why, Mr Watson, that is so kind of you. I'm sure my sister and I would be much obliged," said Cassandra, taking his offered hand and stepping up beside him.

WHAT was her foolish sister doing? George Watson had only been driving the phaeton since the morning. He should at least have to pass a test with an experienced coachman, but sadly even fools like George were allowed out on the roads with no proof they knew one end of a horse from the other.

"Jane?" pleaded Cassandra. They had both promised their mother they would not separate.

The things she did for her sister.

Against her better judgment, Jane scrambled up beside Cassandra. Being only thirteen, she was not considered old enough to need a hand. Acquainted with Jane from her infancy, George probably still thought she rolled down the grassy slope behind the rectory.

Which she did – when no one was watching.

"Tally ho!" George called to his matched pair of horses and flicked the whip. Jane silently calculated how much the carriage would've cost him and came up with a sum that was more than her father earned in a year.

Surprisingly, the ride started well. George kept the horses to a steady pace and avoided the worst of the ruts. Jane began to enjoy herself. Sitting this high, she could see over the hedge to the wheat fields with their knee-high crop. Poppies wound among the stems as butterflies danced above. Maybe George had changed?

But then George had to prove he hadn't changed one little bit. They reached the final approach to the rectory, a stretch of road shaded by elms.

"What say you to making a dashing entrance?" he asked Cassandra.

"Oh no," said Jane. "NO!" she repeated.

"Mr Watson, that would be delightful," agreed Cassandra, elbowing Jane.

With a bark of laughter, George flicked the whip and the phaeton surged forward.

"Cassie!" hissed Jane, clutching Cassandra's arm. "Don't you know your Greek myths?"

Cassandra tore her attention from George for a second. "What are you talking about, Jane?"

"We're in a phaeton! Remember Phaeton: the hero who drove the sun's chariot to disaster?"

"Oh, fiddlesticks."

But even as Cassandra spoke, George gave another crack of the whip. The horses threw caution to the winds and careered around the corner – only to find a drover with his cows blocking the road. The girls screamed, the cows mooed, and George panicked. The carriage veered off the road. The front wheel hit a stone with a jolt that catapulted the passengers from the high seat.

Jane knew briefly, wondrously, what it was like to fly – then landed in a ditch.

OW!

Chapter 2

"Young ladies do not get thrown from phaetons!" declared Mrs Austen, bandaging Cassandra's arm with angry turns of the material.

"I think you'll find that they do," said Jane, pointing to herself and Cassandra. "We just did." Jane's elbow was skinned and her hip bruised but otherwise she was mostly unscathed. The worst impact had been taken by her second-best gown. It was Cassandra who had broken her arm with a snap like a dry twig – though perhaps Jane had only imagined that.

"That's quite enough from you, young lady." Jane was Mrs Austen's least favourite child, as Jane well knew. "Your wit will make you infamous one day."

Jane was hoping for "famous" but infamy sounded exciting.

"And when I said young ladies don't have carriage accidents, I meant that we must never, ever speak of this again. Do not put it in your letters, or your journals." Mrs Austen pursed her lips, a little frown line appearing at the bridge of her Roman nose. "I'll tell your father, of course, when he gets back, but as far as everyone else is concerned, Cassandra has a slight head cold."

"Mama, I have a broken arm!" protested Cassandra.

"No, you do not. You will stay out of sight for the next six weeks while it mends…"

"Colds do not last six weeks!"

"Perhaps we can call it a fever? Yes, that is even better as no one will risk seeing you." She fitted a sling so that Cassandra's left arm was immobilized against her chest. "Because if they see you, they will ask how you broke your arm, and then I will have to admit that I have two daughters with less sense than a gnat – between them!"

Mrs Austen moved to dabbing the cut on Cassandra's forehead. "Whatever possessed the pair of you to accept a drive with George Watson in the first place? If I've told you once, I've told you a thousand times: the squire's son is trouble!"

Jane agreed – in fact, she would capitalize the word in her notebook: TROUBLE. George had clearly been more worried about the damage to his new carriage than to her sister. He had a fit of vapours over mere scratches to the paintwork but showed little concern for the serious injury to Cassandra's arm. For that alone he was now her ENEMY for life. Jane had been sick with concern for Cassandra. She was the dearest person in the world and the only one who understood Jane. Something bad happening to Cassandra was far worse than it happening to herself.

"Just because a young man wants to show off does not mean that you have to agree to be his audience," continued their mother. "And what did we get? My two daughters flying like silly geese from the front seat and near breaking their necks!"

"I did not look like a goose," said Cassandra.

"You did honk," added Jane. "And I fairly flew. We may have looked a little like geese."

"Whose side are you on?" muttered Cassandra.

Jane just smiled. Her sister would know that she was always on her side.

"I don't know what we're going to do," sighed Mrs Austen.

"I rather thought it had already happened," said Jane, rewinding the bandages that Mama had discarded.

"Hush, Jane!" After raising so many children, Mrs Austen had no patience left for her younger daughter. "I meant about the invitation."

"What invitation, Mama?" asked Cassandra.

"I'll mix you some willow bark tea to help with the pain." Mrs Austen packed away her medical supplies.

"Who invited us, and where?" persisted Cassandra.

"*You*, Cassandra. Sir Charles Cromwell and Lady Cromwell have invited you to spend a week at Southmoor Abbey. You were to make yourself useful to Lady Cromwell while they celebrated their son's coming-of-age. But how can you be useful with a broken arm?"

Mama would have been hoping that the favour done for one of the largest landowners in the county would bring advantages to her sons. Girls were useful as cheap tokens to be exchanged in this web of unspoken promises. That meant that Cassandra had dodged a very unattractive week as a slave to Lady Cromwell. Even carriage accidents had a silver lining.

"Jane will go in your place," Mama decided.

WHAT?!

"They won't care as long as one of you turns up the day after tomorrow. They probably won't even notice the exchange."

"Mama!" protested Jane.

"You'd better not fail me, Jane." Mama fixed her with a stare that said she fully expected Jane would disappoint. Jane knew she could never be good enough for her mother – not like Cassandra and her brothers – and that really hurt.

"But I'll need her to look after me!" said Cassandra.

"You have me for that," said Mrs Austen, standing like the herd of cows in the road of Jane's happiness. "Jane, see what you can do to make your third-best gown fit for decent society. You are going to Southmoor Abbey and that is my final word on the subject."

A Page in Mourning

J.A. announces the DEATH of her SECOND-BEST muslin gown. A period of MOURNING will be observed in the Austen household. It will be interred Tuesday next in the rag bag with all due ceremony.

Furthermore, she announces the immediate promotion of her THIRD-BEST to SECOND place. It will immediately INHERIT all duties, responsibilities, etc. etc. of its predecessor.

May God bless it, and all who wear it.

J.A.

Chapter 3

Standing beside her small trunk in the yard of the coaching inn, Jane's spirits sank to her boots. This whole mission was a VERY bad idea. She was going to fail her mother; she just knew it. An Austen girl was simply not cut out to be a companion, not unless that was companion to a brigand or an explorer.

"Oh, Henry," she said to her older brother with a sigh. They were waiting for a servant from the Abbey to collect her.

"Cheer up, Jane! What's the worst that can happen?" Henry was eager to hurry things along as the coach service heading home was due. He was Jane's favourite brother: funny and handsome, having more time to talk to her than the others.

"You really have to ask?"

"You mean you might be too much of an Austen for them?"

To be raised an Austen was to grow up with double the usual dose of daring. Besides Cassandra and herself, there were a lot of boys in the family: Jemmy and Henry both cutting a dash at university, Neddy in Kent, Frank in the navy, and the baby, Charlie, filling the rectory with noise and pranks. (There was also the second-eldest, George, who lived at the farm, but the Austens didn't speak about George.)

Jane's dog, Grandison, sniffed around the door to the tavern, hoping some soft-hearted traveller would throw him a crust.

"I'm going to mess this up – you're all going to hate me!"

He ruffled her hair. "We'd never hate you, Jane. Dislike you a little, maybe."

"Henry!"

He chuckled. "We all love you – for your stories."

"Stop teasing!"

"Actually, I'm not – your stories are wonderful. You might find inspiration where you're going. Don't you know that the Abbey is haunted by an angry ghost? If you see it, you die!" He made a ghostly moan and mimed floating like an apparition.

"Where did you hear that?"

"I spent time at the Abbey too."

"You did?"

"I was sent a few years ago to see if I would get along with the son." Henry wrinkled his brow. "Come to think of it, that must've been when you and Cassandra were away at school in Reading."

"And how did it turn out?"

"I was sent back pretty swiftly, and Mother swore me to secrecy. I was never to mention it again. Oops." He put his hand over his mouth and grinned.

"What happened?"

"I was an abject failure – so you wouldn't be the first."

"But do you think you saw the ghost?"

"I'm still alive, aren't I?"

Jane rolled her eyes.

"No, I didn't. I wanted to hunt for it but I didn't have much time – only managed one minor exploration of the Abbey at night before Cromwell ruined it. We boys didn't get along and I failed to have the calming effect on him that his parents had hoped."

Jane snorted. *Henry? Calming?* That was like taking a hive of bees into your parlour and expecting to take sugared tea undisturbed.

"Sir Charles packed me back home on the first coach out the morning after our adventure. I'm surprised he invited another Austen, but maybe he thinks the female variety will be an improvement?"

"And he would be right."

Henry saluted her for scoring a point. "Are you up for a little ghost-hunting, picking up where I left off? You'll enjoy that, won't you? And it'd make your visit less tedious?"

Jane was famous in the Austen family for her disdain for all things supernatural. "As you well know, I don't believe in ghosts, so I'm unlikely to be bothered by one, Henry."

"They're in the Bible."

"In the Old Testament, and under special circumstances."

He groaned. "Jane, you have no imagination."

She kicked him, as that was the worst thing to say to an Austen, even in jest. "And if I see a ghost, Henry, I'll tell it to get on to heaven – or the other place."

"I do believe you would. Prove there's no such thing as a ghost at the Abbey and I'll give you half a crown." He patted his purse.

Jane thought of the writing paper she could buy with such riches. "You have a deal." She paused, thinking. "What kind of ghost?"

"Uh-ah, that's for me to know and you to find out."

"Ninnyhammer."

"Sneaksby."

They exchanged a few more good-humoured jibes before Grandison caught Henry's attention with his random barks at passing strangers.

"Did you have to bring that mutt with you?" asked Henry.

"I brought Grandison because I needed someone intelligent to talk to on the journey."

Henry grinned.

"And besides, it is perfectly respectable for ladies to travel with their lapdogs."

Henry pointed at Grandison. "That, Jane, is not a lapdog. It is the result of a disgraceful encounter between one of the squire's beagles and what might have been a passing Dalmatian."

"You don't know that!"

"What beagle do you know with black and white spots? I call them spots but perhaps it would be more accurate to think of them as splodges. He has one over his eye like a pirate with an eyepatch, one white ear, one black."

Grandison caught on to the fact that he was being discussed. He looked over at them, tongue lolling in his silly slack-jawed expression.

"He's… unique," said Jane gamely.

"And there's no way anyone will accept he is a lapdog. How on earth could he fit on your lap?"

"His head and front paws do." The rest sprawled behind him, but he had the instincts of a lapdog when he ignored the rules to sit on the sofa with her.

"I can't imagine how Mama was persuaded to let you bring him."

Jane bit her lip.

"Uh-oh. You sly thing!" He looked at her admiringly. Most of the Austens combatted their mother head on; Jane was the only one to have worked out that going around her was best. Henry patted her shoulder. "Don't worry: I won't mention it to Mama. She might not even notice he's missing."

"Thank you." Jane sat down on the trunk, tapping her thigh to summon Grandison. He rewarded her with a lick to the cheek.

A cart clattered into the inn yard, a boy at the reins. He drew up outside the inn door, put on the brake, and jumped to the ground. He disappeared into the inn but emerged a minute later, heading for them.

"Mr Austen?" he asked, touching his cap. He was about Jane's height and age, curly auburn hair and eyes the colour of chestnuts. Whereas Jane was willowy, he was stocky and could probably toss a straw bale without breaking sweat. His plain but good-quality clothes marked him out as a lower servant.

"Yes, that's me," said Henry. "Are you from the Abbey?"

"Yes, sir. I'm here to collect your sister. I was told to expect a pretty dark-haired lady."

"And you've found her." Henry stepped aside to reveal Jane sitting with the dog.

"That's Miss Austen?"

"Yes," said Henry severely.

Jane knew she wasn't as pretty as her older sister: her curly hair was lighter, face redder, hazel eyes just a shade too inquisitive, according to her mother; but normally she was allowed to be a Miss Austen without anyone questioning the fact. She got up.

"This is my trunk – and my dog," she said firmly.

Without another word, the servant heaved the trunk into the back of the cart. He looked at Grandison, then at the front seat, before deciding the dog would have to ride in the rear. He whistled.

"In you go, lad."

Grandison obeyed – something that took Jane by surprise as he always treated her commands as optional. He sat on his haunches, surveying the yard with his cheerful doggy grin.

"Miss?" The boy was now offering Jane help up to the front seat of the cart.

She took his hand and stepped on board.

"Be good, Jane. Make yourself useful," said Henry, dutifully delivering the message Mama had told him to give as final words. He then came closer. "Have fun ghost-hunting. Write it down," he said in a lower tone, "and read it to us when you get back."

Jane smiled. "I will."

Chapter 4

Curious though she was about her destination, particularly the rumours of a ghost, Jane held her peace for the first mile. During that time, the southbound coach service passed them, Henry seated on the roof. He waved his hat and she waved back. Now the dust had settled, she decided she really ought to say something to her driver. She couldn't start with the Abbey ghost, could she?

"What's your name?" she asked instead.

"Luke Tilney, Miss."

"And you're from the Abbey?"

"I work in the stables."

Jane tried to think of a neutral subject. "Do you like horses, Luke?"

"I like them – better than I like most people."

"What's wrong with people?"

"I shouldn't say."

"But I want to know. Please."

He let out a put-upon sigh. "People are generally mean or foolish." He gave her a look that included her in that last group.

"I don't think it's an 'or'," commented Jane.

"Pardon, Miss?" His tone was surly.

"People can be mean *and* foolish – the two usually go together because it is stupid to be mean. Far better to be clever and kind, like my father."

"And who would your father be?"

"The rector of Steventon Parish Church."

Luke snorted as if that explained everything. Jane gave up the subject. Something had soured the boy against his fellow men and a cart ride was not long enough to change his mind.

Grandison decided it was time to join the conversation. He reared up from the back and put his front paws on the seat. He rested his head on Luke's shoulder, drool spilling down the boy's waistcoat front.

"Oh, I'm so sorry," said Jane, pulling out her handkerchief.

Luke waved that away. "I've had much worse on me. What is he? A Dalmatian? No, his shape is all wrong."

"A beagle."

"I know beagles and he's not a beagle."

"A new kind."

Luke nodded as if that settled it. "He's a mongrel."

"Perhaps we aren't entirely sure of his parentage," Jane allowed.

Luke scratched Grandison's ear. "Never mind, lad. I know what that's like. Most pack-masters would put him down at birth. Did you rescue him, Miss?"

"Um..." This was another of those family secrets that her mother insisted everyone never speak of again. When Jane had heard that the squire had ordered the litter be drowned, she'd crept over to the manor barn at night and rescued the surviving puppies. One she'd given to a local shepherd, another to the butcher's boy, but the runt of the litter she'd kept. The squire's servants had known she'd stolen them, of course, but everyone kept quiet for Miss Jane's sake.

"Ah, so you did save him." Luke took a turn through gateposts with pineapples on the plinths. "Lady Cromwell won't let you have him in the house. You send him to me at the stables if she makes a fuss."

"Why would she make a fuss?"

"She has a cat. A great big Persian cat with white fur and evil eyes. How's your dog with cats?" Luke seemed to be warming to her with this discussion of animals.

Jane grimaced. "As you would expect."

"He can stay with me then, if he's turned out of doors."

"Thank you, Luke."

"I'd be doing it for him, not you."

"Understood."
"I don't have time for silly girls."
"Nor do I."
That shut him up.

Chapter 5

The approach to the Abbey wound like a snake through thick woodlands. The house emerged miraculously out of the gentle hills of Hampshire like a castle in a fairy tale. Occupied by monks from the year 1000 until Henry VIII decided to take church property for his own in the sixteenth century, the Abbey still showed signs of its original purpose, with the vaults of a chapel to the left of the main house. There was even a little monkish graveyard – no wonder the locals had got carried away with ghost stories!

The family residence, built soon after the Tudors took over, had three storeys, pierced by narrow windows. A porch dominated the front, and it was all topped by a tawny tiled roof that sprouted a crop of tall brick chimneys. There had to be at least thirty rooms inside. Formal gardens surrounded it, with a ha-ha, or hidden ditch, separating them from the estate lands. Jane could just see a herd of deer roaming a distant pasture. She felt homesick for her whitewashed rectory and vegetable garden that she had helped plant. She'd no more fit in here than a turnip in a row of pineapples. It was going to be awful.

Luke left Jane at the front door and took the cart round to the stable yard. She rang the bell but the butler took his time to answer. First law of being a lady's companion was to expect lax treatment from the staff. Jane sat down on her trunk. They would want to remove her from the step eventually so she might as well wait in comfort.

She took out a little notebook and began a list:

What I know about ghosts

1. They don't exist.

2. But they do appear in tales, plays, etc., even the Old Testament <u>under special circumstances</u>.

3. Henry says there is one here. What kind?

4. To discover –

Footsteps interrupted her note-taking. A young man came from the direction of the stables, whip thwacking against black boots. He was about twenty, hair tied back and unpowdered so it revealed its natural bronze colour. His riding clothes looked like the last word in fashion: tan breeches, well-cut bottle-green coat, frothy white cravat tied with skill. Tucking the notebook away, she rose.

"Good lord, what have we here?" he asked in a pleasant tone. "Are you on the way in or the way out?" He gestured with his whip and Grandison growled. "Easy, boy, I mean no offence. I wouldn't put it past my mother to turn away perfectly good help."

"I'm Miss Austen," said Jane. "I've come to be a companion to Lady Cromwell for the week."

"Henry Austen's sister?"

Jane nodded.

"In that case, please forgive the reception you've been given." He thumped on the door. "Parks! Parks! There's a damsel in distress at the door."

A short but stout man hurried to open the door. "Master Cromwell, so sorry for my tardiness. A little emergency in the library: your mother's cat got stuck on the Caesar bookshelf."

"Not again! You know the dashed pest always finds its way down eventually."

"But your mother..."

"Quite." Cromwell sighed. "Parks, this is Miss Austen. I believe she's expected?"

Jane decided this was not the moment to explain how in fact she was not the Miss Austen who was expected, but a lesser version sent in her sister's place to "be useful".

The butler gave Jane a shallow nod. "Miss Austen, I'll have a maid show you to your room."

Cromwell passed his whip to the butler, then turned back to Jane. He took her hand and kissed it. "One damsel rescued. Miss Austen, until later."

Oh my, thought Jane. He was charming. Why had Henry not liked him? It was a good job that it was she rather than Cassandra who had come. Cassandra would have already lost her head over the handsome heir of the Cromwells. A romantic, her sister would imagine him falling hopelessly in love with the penniless gentleman's daughter and casting himself and his fortune at her feet after an exciting courtship in which he proved his devotion despite numerous rebuffs. Jane was far too practical for such daydreams.

"This way, Miss Austen," said Parks, giving her dog a doubtful look. "Er..."

"Yes?"

"Never mind for the moment. This way."

What had he been about to say? wondered Jane.

Jane was given a room on the topmost floor. Situated at the front, it had a fine view over the carriage approach and the stables partially hidden by trees to the left, but it was in size a servant's room. She suspected that it might once have belonged to a former governess of the Abbey's children. A little bookshelf of dull educational works supported this conclusion.

Still, it was a room of her own, and a place where she could expect to remain undisturbed. She flopped on the bed, making the springs creak; Grandison curled up on the rag rug by the small hearth, perfectly content.

They were both about to fall into a doze when a loud argument erupted in the corridor outside – but in a language Jane did not recognize.

Rolling off the bed, she crept to the door and opened it a crack. A girl dressed in an orange robe was shouting at an older man in a white apron. Both had skin the colour of cinnamon, dark eyes and hair. From the family resemblance, they had to be father and daughter. With a swell of excitement, Jane realized where they were from.

INDIA!

She had only ever seen people from that country in pictures. How perfectly wonderful!

The girl shook her head at the much taller man, her tone of complaint needing no translation. The man – a cook by the uniform – argued back, gesturing with wide sweeps of his hands. Jane translated that as "What can I do about it?". It was at this point that Grandison decided to see what he could do to calm them down. He slipped past Jane and bounded toward the pair with his "there's nothing a game of chase can't cure" approach. Unfortunately, his suggestion was misunderstood. The man swept the girl behind him and pulled a knife from his belt. Confused, Grandison ground to a halt, backed up, and growled.

The man took a step forward.

No one – and Jane meant NO ONE – threatened her dog!

Jane stepped into the corridor. "Put that away. He only wants to play," she said, grabbing Grandison's collar.

The knife disappeared. The man bowed, hands held together at his chest. "Miss."

A second behind him, his daughter copied his gesture.

"Is anything the matter?" Jane asked, alluding as delicately as she could to their row. She'd give her best bonnet to find out what that had been about.

"Everything is perfect," said the man, in his musical accent that made the words sound poetic.

She didn't believe that for one moment. "I see."

The man bowed again. He was waiting for her to dismiss him. Even she, a girl visitor, outranked the staff.

"Oh, er, carry on," Jane said.

The man disappeared into a room two doors down, his daughter only a step behind. Just before she closed the door, the girl glanced back. She had fine dark eyes, a little like a deer glimpsed in a thicket. She was probably wondering what one of the "quality" was doing up in the attics. Jane smiled and the puzzlement deepened.

"I'm Jane," said Jane.

The girl closed the door.

The Letter S

Salutations, Sister 'Ssandra!

Swift & short sending to state survival of sensiblest sister Steventon to Southmoor safe & secure. Society seems scintillating with self-assured son, stocky servants, & secretive subcontinental strangers.

Our senior sibling swore Southmoor swarming with spectres to spook sister. She seeks signs of silliness of such spirits, staking several shillings on success.

Send yr sister stacks of suggestions to show stories be but soapsuds.

Speak soon.

Sincerely yr Servant Sister

Chapter 6

J ane allowed herself an hour's rest before heading downstairs to report for duty. She decided to err on the side of caution and leave Grandison in her room. If Lady Cromwell was usually accompanied by her bookcase-climbing Persian, it would not be good to begin with a cat-and-dog fight.

Her "S" note to Cassandra in her pocket (how the family would chuckle over that!), Jane arrived in the entrance hall. This was possibly one of the oldest parts of the Abbey: thick stone walls, hammer beam roof, white plasterwork. She could imagine Elizabethan noblemen striding through like characters from her favourite Shakespeare plays. There was a stuffed bear standing guard in one alcove. Unable to resist, she curled her hands into claws and growled a challenge at it.

The butler, carrying a tray of cups, appeared from a room to her right. Embarrassed, Jane clasped her hands behind her back. Young ladies like her would never dream of growling at stuffed bears, oh no, *never*.

"Lady Cromwell?" Jane asked.

Parks put the tray down on a side table. "Allow me to introduce you, Miss. Please follow me."

Jane took out her note and left it on the silver salver for the postboy to collect. Following the butler, she entered a parlour, walls coloured damson, drapes red with a gold fringe – the combined effect was like taking up residence inside a giant plum. A painted screen stood to one side of the fire, an intriguing scene of Chinamen scampering over a bridge. On the other side of the hearth a woman sat in a winged chair, head lolling, lace cap askew, yellow curls dangling. She was dressed in a printed calico petticoat with an open-fronted gown. Jane couldn't quite make out the design but it looked at a distance like twisted foliage and flowers. She would have to take notes for her sister and mother. It was always good to keep up with fashion even if you couldn't afford it yourself.

A white cat jumped up, sprawled possessively across the back of the armchair, and hissed. Jane took a step back. The Persian.

Parks cleared his throat. "My lady, Miss Austen has arrived."

The lady's head jerked upright, revealing soft blue eyes.

"Parks?" said the lady.

"The rector's daughter, my lady. Miss Austen."

"Henry's sister? We were expecting her today?" Her voice was reed thin; Jane would have anticipated a deep alto to emerge from that chest.

"We were, ma'am."

"Cassandra?" Lady Cromwell's eyes turned to Jane.

Jane bobbed a curtsey. "No, ma'am. My sister has a fever. My mother sent me in her place. My name is Jane."

"Jane Austen? What am I to do with a *Jane* Austen? Jane is so plain. I was expecting your sister. At least her name is suited to the best company."

Jane sighed at the reminder that she was the least of the Austen brood – the second, less pretty daughter with the unremarkable name. Surrounded by loving family though she was, she knew that in the world's estimation she was of no earthly use to anyone. It made it hard to believe in herself at times, like right now, when she felt so very unwelcome.

The lady turned back to the butler. "And the tea was too strong, Parks."

"Of course, my lady. I will ask the housekeeper to take more care in future."

Lady Cromwell beckoned Jane forward and handed her a sewing basket. "Fix it," she said. "Parks, have you seen my son?"

Fix it? The lady spoke to her like a slave! Fuming, Jane sat on a low stool and glared at the tangle of threads. From the white hairs caught among the colours, she suspected that the wretched Persian liked playing with silks. She would have to cure it of that or she would be repeating this task every day. As if summoned by her thoughts, the cat leaped down from the back of the chair and prowled closer. There was something cold about the feline stare, like that of a little goddess with a grudge against humanity.

The cat scratched at the basket.

"Muffin, leave it alone," said Lady Cromwell lazily.

Muffin? It should be Kali or Sinbad. Jane bared her teeth at the Persian. The cat scowled but didn't come any closer. Turing around once, it sat down and washed its paw as if nothing had passed between them.

"My point," muttered Jane, winding a scarlet silk on to a card. She made a note as she would if keeping score during a game of cards.

Jane 1, Muffin 0

The door banged open, and Jane dropped her thread. An older man strode into the parlour, hunting rifle in hand. He had the tea-coloured skin of a person who spent much of the summer outdoors, dark hair with wings of white at the temples, and hard brown eyes. He moved with a commanding gait that left you in no doubt he owned everything and everyone in the room. Enter Sir Charles.

Jane rose and bobbed a curtsey.

"Parks, sack the housemaids! There's a puddle in the hall and I damn nearly slid to my death in it."

Jane had a sudden fear that Grandison had somehow escaped her bedroom. Was that a distant bark she could hear? *Oh no!*

Parks paled. "Of course, Sir Charles."

"If that was your cat, Sophia, I'll ring her neck."

"Oh, Charles, don't joke!" fluttered Lady Cromwell.

"I'm not joking. I'll shoot the creature that did it." He collapsed into the biggest chair in the room and crossed his mud-splattered boots at the ankle, gun across his knees. "Fetch tea and brandy. And cakes. Has Arjun been baking today?"

"Yes, sir," said Parks.

"Then bring the spicy ones. None of this plain sponge nonsense. Might as well eat cotton fluff."

"Yes, sir." The butler hovered.

"At once, Parks!"

"Yes, sir." The butler scurried out, moving fast for a man who was almost as round as he was tall.

Sir Charles looked around for a footstool but Jane was in occupation. "Who's the child?"

"This is the girl from Steventon," said Lady Cromwell. "The one you wanted to keep me out of trouble this week, dearest."

"She's not as handsome as I remember."

"That's her sister. They have two. Mrs Austen sent the younger one – Jane."

"*Jane*?" It appeared Sir Charles shared his wife's prejudice against plain Christian names. "You're blocking my stool, Miss Jane."

Jane wondered if she had ever met a ruder man. "Of course, sir." She stepped aside and took the basket of silks to an upright chair by a little round table.

"It is going to be a busy week: you'll keep company with my wife, I trust?" continued Sir Charles.

"As you wish, sir." The scarlet thread was neatly wound. Jane moved on to the blue.

"She never rises before noon, so you will have your mornings to yourself."

"Oh, Charles, you make me sound quite a slugabed!" tittered Lady Cromwell.

"Do you like horses, girl?" Sir Charles said in a sudden change of subject.

Jane thought of the old sway-backed horse her father sometimes hired for the Austen sisters to ride.

"I know very little about them," she admitted.

"Pity. You'll soon learn that a string of good hunters is worth more to an estate than any number of mealy-faced ancestors in their gold frames." He pointed at a particularly pinch-nosed lady who glared at them from above the mantelpiece.

"You shouldn't speak of my forebears so, my dear. My husband loves his horses," added Lady Cromwell for Jane's benefit. "I sometimes think if it were a choice between his family and his stables, he'd move in with them."

Sir Charles gave her a humourless smile. "So witty, my love."

"Are you still intending to give Wicky the two-year-old for his birthday?"

"A more promising mare I've never seen," Sir Charles said with a sigh. "The boy will ruin her in a year."

"But are you?" pressed Lady Cromwell, showing she could develop a spine when it came to something involving her son.

"You shouldn't have told him that I was raising her as a coming-of-age gift. You've tied my hands." He made a restless gesture of pulling them apart.

"I'm so pleased." The lady relaxed back into her armchair. "He was worried you might've changed your mind after that trouble last month. You know that was all Fitzwilliam's fault. He should've stepped in before it went too far."

Parks entered, followed by a footman carrying a laden tray. Jane's face brightened when she saw that a cup and plate had been included for her. The butler began serving.

"I caught that mechanical boy at it again," said Sir Charles. He crammed a little round cake into his mouth, speaking through his food. "I ordered the head groom to tan his hide."

"Caught whom, dear?" asked Lady Cromwell, wrinkling her nose at the offered plate. "Is there jam sponge today, Parks? This foreign stuff upsets my digestion."

"*Mysore pak*, flavoured with cardamom!" declared Sir Charles, smacking his lips.

"Of course, my lady." The butler offered her a second salver.

"Which boy were you talking about, dear? There are so many running about the place," said Lady Cromwell.

"The Tilney boy, the one I took in when his mother died. We couldn't find out who the father was, remember? He works in the stables." He was talking about Luke!

"I don't notice the stableboys. What did he do?" asked Lady Cromwell.

"I'm sure I told you about him before. The lad is mad about machines. If you give him an old clock, he'll have it apart in five minutes flat and mend it in ten."

"I'm sure you did the right thing." Annoyingly, Lady Cromwell did not ask for more details.

"No gratitude: that's what annoys me." Sir Charles slurped his tea as Parks silently placed a plate and cup beside Jane. He'd put one of each kind of cake out for her. She smiled her thanks.

"I might turn him off – but then who would mend the clocks?" mused Sir Charles.

Jane had only met Luke briefly, but that sounded very bad for him. "If you don't mind me asking, sir, what did he do?"

Sir Charles turned to look at her in surprise. It was like one of the portraits had suddenly addressed him. "What's it to you?"

"I'm just curious, sir."

"Curiosity is a vice in a young female."

Jane lowered her gaze. There went her plans to ask him later about the ghost!

"The boy built some infernal device – in the tack room of all places. He calls it a steam engine – claims it is the future. I've never heard such rot!"

Jane knew about these new machines from her father. Mines in Cornwall had been using them for some years.

"It is quite impressive, to have built a miniature one out of spare pipes and things he has begged off the blacksmith, but the fire risk! In my tack room! One cinder and a thousand pounds worth of saddles and halters would go up in smoke." Sir Charles reached for another cake. "So, naturally, I had the device removed and ordered him to be soundly beaten. Another offence like that and I'll turn him out on the road."

Hysterical barking erupted in the hallway.

Oh no. No, no, no, no, no!

"What's that racket?" asked Sir Charles, grabbing his gun.

Outside, men shouted and girls screamed. The parlour door was nosed open and Grandison trotted merrily through the breach, making a beeline for Jane. Leaping up, Sir Charles raised his gun and aimed.

Chapter 7

"Stop!" Jane shouted, throwing herself between gun and dog.

"Out of the way, girl!" bellowed Sir Charles.

A young man who had been chasing Grandison lunged for the dog's collar but missed. Grandison, unaware he was in mortal danger, danced around, greeting Lady Cromwell, who shrieked in terror, spilling tea and cake, much to the dog's delight. He turned his attention to the crumbs on the carpet. Muffin saw her chance: she pounced from the chairback and clawed at Grandison's nose. With a surprised yelp, he retreated behind the sofa, shivering. Jane threw her arms around him and refused to let go. He was a trigger-pull away from death and didn't know it!

WORST moment of her life!

"Fitzwilliam, what's the meaning of this?" asked Sir Charles, cutting across the confusion.

Jane stared up in desperate appeal to the young man. He was tall, with a crop of dark curls, about the age of their son, Cromwell. Dressed too fine for a servant, he had the air of a low-ranking gentleman, a tutor or schoolmaster. He wasn't conventionally handsome – a little too angular for that. At the moment, he might be all that stood between Grandison and death.

The young man turned to Sir Charles apologetically. "A dog got loose in the kitchens, sir."

"I can see that for myself. But we don't have dogs indoors. Everyone knows that." Sir Charles aimed the gun again, but how he was going to fire without hitting her, Jane did not know, for she was not budging. Perhaps he didn't care?

The man gave her an anxious look. "Not everyone. It's the young lady's dog, sir. Parks was going to speak to her about the rules later, but as she had only just arrived, he had not yet had an opportunity. We had no idea it would get in here."

Jane swallowed. "His name is Grandison, and he's my lapdog."

"Get rid of it," said Sir Charles, finally lowering his gun.

Shaken, Jane grasped Grandison's collar and moved before anyone else could be given the task. She didn't like Sir Charles's idea of getting rid of things. "At once, sir. I apologize. I did not know about the rule."

Sir Charles set the gun down. "My wife has a mortal fear of dogs. One mistake I can overlook, Miss Austen. Two, and you'll be put on a coach like your brother, straight back to your little rectory."

Dragging Grandison with her, Jane left the parlour and propelled the reluctant dog out into the hall. Parks was waiting and opened the front door for them.

"Thank you, Parks."

"You're welcome, Miss. I'm sorry I didn't say anything earlier, but I'd already left you waiting on the doorstep…"

"I understand."

As she passed through she saw a maid was cleaning up a puddle by the doorpost. Grandison had at least tried to get outside. He didn't normally have accidents. That too was her fault.

"Grandison, you are ruining everything," Jane said in exasperation, though she knew who really was to blame. She was.

Now outside, Grandison's spirits lifted and he cocked a leg against a planter by the front door.

Jane slapped her forehead. "Not there! Do you have no discretion?"

He grinned at her and bounded in the wrong direction.

"Not that way!" Jane put two fingers in her mouth and whistled.

"Good heavens, I didn't know ladies could do that." Fitzwilliam had arrived at her shoulder.

Jane refused to feel embarrassed. "Brothers can be useful teachers."

"I thought you might need help, but now I'm not so sure." He really did have a pleasant face, a humorous expression in his eyes, even if he looked like he rarely smiled. "That must have been terrifying for you."

"Thank you for what you did in there."

"It was nothing."

"Would he really have shot my dog?"

"I wish I could say no."

"Then I'm taking Grandison to the stables."

"I'll show you the way."

The only problem with that plan was that Grandison had spotted the deer in the distance and looked intent on asking them to play. He stood, one front leg curled off the ground, nose pointing in the direction he wished to go. He bolted.

"GRANDISON!" Jane would never get him back now.

"Here, boy!" Fitzwilliam took a cricket ball from his pocket.

Grandison stopped dead in his tracks. Deer, ball? Deer, ball? They could both see the doggy calculation.

Fitzwilliam sealed the deal by throwing the ball in the right direction. With a happy bound, Grandison dashed after it.

"A simple creature," Fitzwilliam remarked.

"Yes." And he was far too simple to have plotted an escape from her room unaided. So how had Grandison got out of her room? She remembered closing the door behind her. Someone had to have let him out. But why? To make trouble for her? To poke around in her things?

Jane resolved to make sure her writings were well hidden in future. There might be an enemy in the house.

"We didn't have time to introduce ourselves. I'm Edward Fitzwilliam, son of Sir Charles's steward." He gave her a little bow.

That solved the mystery of his role: stewards managed the land for the landowner, rather like a captain commanding a ship for the merchant who owned it. Jane bobbed a curtsey. "Jane Austen, younger daughter of the rector of Steventon."

"Pleased to meet you, Miss Austen. Are you with us long?"

"Not long. I'm here to look after Lady Cromwell this week."

"You'll be sent home after the ball?" He opened a gate for her and stood back to let her go through first.

"I think so. I'm not really in charge of my movements."

"Few of us are," he said with a hint of bitterness. "This is a close-knit family; they tend not to keep strangers around for long."

"For only so long as we're useful?"

"More that it's just so hard for them to keep up appearances in front of those who might carry bad reports abroad."

Jane wondered what he had in mind that the family might wish to keep hidden. "Would that be because they don't want strangers to find out about the ghost?" The words tumbled unbidden from her mouth.

He turned an amused face to her. "What ghost is that, Miss Austen?"

She would kill her brother! "It is only that I'd heard that, maybe, the Abbey was haunted?"

"If gullible people claim they've seen such a thing, they do not carry tales to me."

And didn't Jane feel foolish? Henry would get a frog in his bed when she returned home.

"And I have to warn you against exploring the ruins on the strength of such rumours. They're not safe and Sir Charles has ordered no one to go there without an approved guide."

"Not safe?"

"Falling stones, uneven ground – Cromwell broke his collarbone climbing on the walls with another boy a few years ago, in some night-time dare or other that went wrong."

That had to be the cause of Henry's sudden return home. It was exactly like him to go ghost-hunting at night. He would think nothing of scaling perilous walls in the dark – even think it a great adventure. That streak ran in the Austen family.

Seeing the stables ahead, Jane remembered that Sir Charles had ordered Luke be beaten. *This might not be a good time to ask him for a favour.*

Chapter 8

Grandison dropped the cricket ball at Fitzwilliam's feet and looked up expectantly.

"Not now, boy." Fitzwilliam slipped a length of twine under the dog's collar as a makeshift lead.

The dog wagged his tail, taking disappointment in his stride.

"He makes an excellent lapdog," said Fitzwilliam.

"I always thought so," agreed Jane.

"For a giant." Jane could tell by his tone that she was amusing him.

"I'm tall for my age."

A man emerged from the nearest doorway and nodded deferentially to Fitzwilliam. "Master Fitzwilliam."

"Mr Scroop. Miss Austen's dog needs a place to stay."

"Luke Tilney offered to look after him," Jane ventured, as the man didn't look the sort to care much for someone else's animals.

"Call Luke for us, would you, Mr Scroop?" said Fitzwilliam.

"He's not feeling well, sir… if you understand me," said the head groom.

Oh no, the beating must've already taken place. Poor Luke!

"But a visit from this dog might cheer him. Where is he?" said Fitzwilliam bracingly.

"In the loft over Romeo's stall. He's there to guard the horse at night in case of thieves – Sir Charles's orders."

"And Luke pulled the short straw as usual? I know the way. Please, go about your duties."

Fitzwilliam waited until Scroop retreated. From the expression on his face, he didn't much like the head groom.

Jane felt in the little bag that hung from her waistband – her pocket for essential treasures like her notebook. There was a little twist of paper at the bottom.

"I think Luke's just been whipped," she said in a low voice.

"Sadly, that's not unusual. If anything goes wrong at the stables, Luke is usually blamed."

"Sir Charles said he endangered the tack room with one of his machines."

"Ah. I've warned Luke that his contraptions aren't appreciated here."

"And some men don't like it when they find other people might be cleverer than them," Jane muttered.

"What's that?"

"Nothing."

He looked at her doubtfully. "Something tells me that you will grow up to be a dangerous woman, Miss Austen."

"Oh, dangerous! That is quite the best compliment anyone has paid me. Thank you."

She would write it down later: DANGEROUS!

He laughed. It was like a glimpse of sunshine through a thick forest canopy. Jane felt proud of herself having been the cause.

They entered the stall belonging to Sir Charles's prize stallion. Romeo turned his head from the hay-filled manger and snickered a welcome. Black as a starless night and glossy like a guardsman's boots, he was quite the most magnificent horse Jane had ever seen. If only she had a carrot to offer.

"Luke, visitors!" called Fitzwilliam.

Jane heard a scuffling from above and a pale face appeared at the top of a ladder.

"Mr Fitzwilliam?"

"The young lady's dog has been banished from the house. She said you'd look after him for her."

"I did." The boy climbed slowly down the ladder, moving with none of his usual grace.

Fitzwilliam put a gentle hand on his shoulder. "All right, Luke?"

He nodded.

Jane held out the twist of paper she'd retrieved from her pocket. Luke looked at it in confusion.

"What's that?"

"Barley sugar. I find it helps when I'm feeling… poorly." She chose her words carefully.

He kept his hands down. "I can't take charity from you, Miss."

"Oh, come now, Luke." Fitzwilliam plucked the candy from her palm and held it out. "A kind young lady offers you a little sugar medicine – it would be ungentlemanly to turn her down."

Luke glanced up at Fitzwilliam. "Really?"

"Yes."

Luke took the sweet. "Thank you, Miss."

"What's all this?" Cromwell walked into the stable. "A party – and I wasn't invited?" He nodded to her. "Miss Austen, you've fallen among thieves, I see," he teased.

Jane suddenly remembered that the son of the house had seen her take in her dog on arrival. Why had he not warned her of his parents' rules?

Grandison sniffed Cromwell's leg. Cromwell scratched him behind the ears.

"He can smell my hounds. I keep them in the kennels as Mother can't abide them. What's all this about your latest invention, Luke? Papa said you've created a fire hazard?"

Luke perked up at the mention. "I did, sir. Not the hazard," he quickly corrected, "but a little engine."

Cromwell slapped him on the back. "Good work."

Luke winced.

"Don't worry, I asked Parks to rescue it. I told my father it's too fine to destroy. He's now planning to display it to the scientifically minded gentlemen at my birthday ball."

"Thank you, sir."

"But Scroop took his rod to you already?"

Luke nodded. He was looking everywhere but at Jane.

"That sounds like Pa. Punish you for something but be completely happy to use it to his own advantage."

"I wouldn't know, sir. Sir Charles is very generous." Luke sounded as if the words choked him.

"With my mother's fortune – and when spent on these horses – he'll go to extraordinary lengths, as we all know; otherwise, I'm afraid to say, he can be quite the penny-pincher. Wouldn't you agree, Fitzwilliam?"

Jane's new friend joined Luke in looking embarrassed. "Not my place to judge the baronet, Cromwell."

"Yes, but why are you here, Fitz, and not at university? He promised your father he'd see to your education, didn't he?"

Jane, with her own clutch of brothers, knew when someone was putting in the knife. Cromwell's charm was disappointingly shallow, like a silver-plated blade, the thin layer already rubbing off.

"I'm sure your father will remember his promises to me in the fullness of time."

"In the fullness of never." Cromwell was in an odd, out-of-sorts mood, thought Jane. "Still, this is supposed to be my birthday week and we should leave such dismal subjects behind. Luke, why don't you show us the rest of your little devices?"

Jane worried that Luke would resent being forced into displaying his private hobby, but, fortunately, he looked pleased.

"This way, sirs. Miss Austen."

Chapter 9

Grandison fell into adoring step with Luke as they headed to the other side of the yard to the tack room. The workbench was clear of clutter, the halters and saddles hung neatly on the walls. Luke reached underneath, pulled out a box, and began laying out his treasures. Most of them were toys: a wind-up windmill, an acrobat on a wire, a marching soldier; others Jane thought might be little clockwork machines. In places she could see what parts Luke had scrounged – a clock spring here, a pocket watch chain there – but mostly the pieces had been handcrafted. It would've taken great dedication to file, grind, and solder his inventions.

"How do you know how to do all this?" marvelled Jane.

Luke shrugged. "I borrow books from Mr Fitzwilliam's father – and I take things apart."

"You can read scientific works?"

He looked offended by her question. "Of course! Mr Fitzwilliam Senior makes sure all the servants can read."

Jane touched the acrobat and he spun on his wire, doing a handstand before flopping back down.

"That was the first one I made," said Luke. "It works on a simple pivot. I made another version but a visitor bought it for a shilling."

"And this?" Jane touched a black metal box.

"A clockwork knife grinder, but I'm having trouble with it." He lifted the lid to show the groove where the blade should rest. "It's grinding unevenly. I need to fix that. I wonder…" His eyes took on a speculative glaze as his brain sorted through new possibilities.

Luke would be much happier working as an apprentice to a clockmaker, or in one of the new factories, thought Jane. "These are very clever."

"Our Luke is a genius," said Cromwell. "Papa thinks Luke just makes toys. People like Papa are oblivious to the signs that the future is going to be very different."

"In what way different?" she asked.

He looked pleased to be asked. "Things are changing."

"Oh?" said Jane encouragingly.

Cromwell folded his arms and leaned on the workbench. He was caught in a shaft of light, which glinted from his burnished mop of hair; he looked like an archangel in a church window. "After the American revolution, people won't stand for being ruled by the landowners; they'll want a say in how the country is run, especially the new men, the merchants, the shippers, the factory owners. I for one can't wait to see what the next century will bring."

Jane thought of her father in his black robes and clerical collar sitting in his study, looking out on a tranquil garden. Mr Austen often spoke of the virtues of slow change, careful improvements, respect for traditions, a life of humble faith in God. "But wouldn't that be dangerous, to change the way things have been done without knowing the outcome?"

"Oh yes, Miss Austen, but shaking up the puzzle, throwing the pieces in the air, that's exciting, isn't it?"

"Sounds like a way to lose pieces, if you ask me."

He gave her a patronizing smile that made her want to kick him. "Ladies, of course, are not expected to understand the need for change."

Jane felt insulted. "I like change too – just the right sort."

"And who decides what's the right sort? That's what's going to change."

Jane was soon to learn that a great change was coming to Southmoor faster than any of them then knew.

She spent the rest of the day in the plum parlour with Lady Cromwell. Outside, the June day clouded over so the lady could not be tempted to take a turn around the garden. She passed her time fretting at her embroidery, no stitch going quite as she liked. Jane had to admit that Lady Cromwell was skilled with the needle; her depiction of a bowl of fruit was very lifelike.

While she stitched, Lady Cromwell kept on a monologue of nothings that Jane was invited to encourage with the occasional interjection – a "yes, my lady", a "no, my lady", or a "well, I never". The only way Jane could stand the boredom was to play a game, using each one in turn even if not entirely fitting to the context. The lady did not seem to notice. Jane had managed two rounds when Lady Cromwell turned to the subject of their cook.

"Of course, Sir Charles was spoiled by the diet in Madras with the Company. It is curry this, curry that, never a plain pudding or honest piece of boiled meat," said Lady Cromwell.

"The Company" meant the East India Company. It controlled British trade with the Far East and kept a private army to defend its interests. Jane's family often debated whether it was a good thing or not. Her father feared that the Company was getting too powerful, like a self-governing state all of its own, avoiding the rules set by governments. Her brothers, though, supported it, as it offered the promise of riches when no other way could be found. Any young man without a fortune, any second son without prospects, or a well-born girl without suitors would set off to India in hopes some of the riches the Company had would pass to them. It was interesting, thought Jane, that Sir Charles had felt the desire to travel that far as there were no signs he needed the money.

"He had to bring back that Hindoo cook, Arjun," continued Lady Cromwell. "Since then, I've not had a decent meal in this house. Have you seen him?"

"Yes, my lady," said Jane, pleased to have the right interjection at hand.

"An odd-looking fellow."

Jane had thought him handsome.

"I'm sure he'll poison us one day as he hates us all. Didn't you fear for your life when you ate your dinner, Jane?"

"No, my lady," said Jane truthfully. The almond chicken dish had been tasty, the saffron rice a delight.

"I suppose a girl like you doesn't have the delicate digestion of one of my blood," mused Lady Cromwell. She made it sound like Jane regularly dined on scraps in the pig pail. "But Sir Charles won't hear any argument on the subject. He refuses to give up the cook, or send him back as the man asks. He's not happy here."

"Well, I never," said Jane.

"I know!" Lady Cromwell nodded, aghast at the cheek of it. "Fancy not wanting to remain in England! He wants to swap this for what? A dusty city somewhere far on the other side of the world where they have snakes in the houses!"

The lady's characterization of Arjun's home was lacking in something. What was it? Oh yes: FIRST-HAND KNOWLEDGE. India had a very long history and culture all of its own about which to be proud. And Jane was sure they had their snake problem under control.

"You wouldn't turn your back on a position in this household, would you, Jane, if you were in his shoes?"

Jane bit her lip. Her answers had wrongly aligned. "Yes?"

"Yes? Yes, you would turn your back?" The lady put down her needle. "No?"

"That's what I thought you meant. That cook doesn't know which side his bread is buttered on."

Jane doubted very much he ate buttered bread. He probably cooked up some fantastic oriental delight like the cake she had sampled earlier.

"Complaining because his wife and twin sons are still in Madras! But I won't have more of them here. At least his daughter can make herself useful in the laundry."

"Well, I never." Jane was losing heart for her private game. It sounded so sad: a family parted by thousands of miles. How far was it to India? A voyage of many months at least.

"I know that Sir Charles did say the cook could send for them once the boys had grown old enough, but I never promised such a thing. They must be five now and Arjun wants them to join him. But I've put my foot down and told Sir Charles the house had quite enough Hindoos. Where to draw the line? Next they'd want to move in their elephant and their monkeys."

That actually sounded quite splendid: a house of exotic animals!

"It's only natural that the cook will want his sons – boys are so much more special to a father than girls – but this way he'll have to go back to join them and I can employ a decent English cook." She snipped off an end of thread and admired the strawberry she had just embroidered. "It's the only way to manage men, Jane: so they don't know they are doing what you want."

"Yes, my lady." Jane had to admire the lady's manoeuvres. She might not be the most intelligent woman, but she had a talent for a low kind of cunning.

Chapter 10

Lying in bed that night, missing Cassandra, Jane thought about the little family down the corridor. Lady Cromwell had barely mentioned the girl but she must be missing her mother. Jane counted out the years they'd been here on her fingers. The twins were five so Arjun had been brought back with Sir Charles fairly recently. It was very unusual for a man in Sir Charles's station as a landowner to travel so far.

That oddity was worth noting down to ask her father later. What would take Sir Charles so far from home?

Throwing back the covers, Jane got up and lit a candle to make her note. As she stood at the desk by the window, she caught a glimpse between the gap in the ill-fitting curtains of a light moving outside.

The Abbey ghost!

Pushing the drape aside, she looked out into the pitch black of a moonless night. Her eyes adjusted and she could see a little by starlight: the silhouette of the trees and the stable weathercock against the constellation-stippled sky, the gleam of the pale gravel on the carriageway. A lantern appeared from the direction of the stables and bobbed closer. It looked like it was floating in mid-air.

Be sensible, Jane. It might look ghostly but there would be a perfectly logical explanation. A nightwatchman? Jane pressed her forehead against the cold pane, trying to make out more details, but all she could see was the outline of a full-length cloak and deep hood, distinctly monastic.

The lantern-carrier passed the front door and glided on to the far side of the house, heading toward the forbidden ruins.

No wonder there were rumours of a ghost if people were allowed to wander about at night in such a mysterious manner! Jane felt angry because she was aware of a traitorous inkling that it might be a real apparition.

Should she follow? But by the time she got her boots on and ran downstairs, the lantern-bearer might be long gone. Also, Fitzwilliam had warned her off the ruins. She should be cautious and at least have a look at them by daylight before gadding about them in the dark. Almost being shot was enough adventure for one day. With a sigh, Jane got back into bed, good sense prevailing over Austen impulsiveness. She promised herself to be better prepared tomorrow night. Henry's prize money would be hers.

The next day, after fitful sleep, Jane rose early and fetched Grandison so that she could visit the ruins before anyone else stirred. Grandison was her excuse: if caught, she could claim she merely followed him in.

"Good boy," she whispered to the dog, slipping off the leash. "Go play."

He bounded with disobedient zeal into the ruins, wriggling with no trouble under the rope that barred the entrance.

"Oh my!" said Jane, for the benefit of any onlooker. "Now I must go save my dog. What a blow."

Keeping her distance from the walls, she made a circuit of the ruins. There was no trace of the night visitor, not even footsteps in the dew.

A ghost wouldn't leave tracks, whispered the more lurid side of her imagination.

That's quite enough of that, she told herself.

The ruined Abbey was picturesque: fallen columns, most walls only up to her waist, rocky outlines of the buildings that had once stood there – bakery, brewhouse, and infirmary. The most complete part was the chapel. This had no roof now and grass grew on the ground among the last of the flagstones and tiles. The turf was springy and smooth underfoot like a bowling green. She found it hard to believe that there was anything especially unsafe about the ruins. If she owned them, she would open them to the public, not rope off the entrance and post signs forbidding entry as Sir Charles had done.

Jane pressed her luck as far as she thought wise on this first visit. As she headed back to the stables with her dog, a string of gaily painted wagons rolled into sight. She had heard during the embroidery session that Cromwell had requested a party with sporting competitions for the tenants on his actual birthday. A ball for the local gentry would be held a day later on Saturday – this last his parents' idea, as they were hoping to marry him off like a prince in a fairy tale. Lady Cromwell spent nearly an hour telling Jane all the finer points of her ballgown. Jane had scribbled these down for her letter home. Cassandra and her mother would love the details and possibly try some of the easier alterations on their own dresses at the next dance in Steventon.

Jane noticed she hadn't been invited to the ball. She imagined the (un)invitation.

Sir Charles and Lady Cromwell

DO NOT request the pleasure of

Miss Jane Austen's company

on the occasion of their son's coming-of-age ball.

Dress – not required. Ditto carriages.

DO NOT be at Southmoor Abbey summer ballroom,

8 p.m., 27th June, 1789.

P.S. Stay in your room.

P.P.S. Your name is too plain for polite company in any case.

Returning to the stables past the laundry room, Jane came across the Indian girl wrestling with a sheet against a stiff breeze. Jane hurried forward and caught an end just before it came to grief.

"Here, let me help." She lifted up the damp bundle so the girl could flip it over the line. "This is really a two-girl job."

The girl just looked at her.

"Do you speak English?"

"Deepti!" called a woman from inside the wash house. "Are you bothering the guest?" A large woman with muscled arms bustled out with another loaded basket in her embrace.

"She's not bothering me," Jane said. "I offered to help. Nothing worse than mud on a clean sheet." Speaking of which, Jane checked what had happened to Grandison. He was likely to choose this moment to shake himself, spraying water from his dip in a muddy puddle over all this lovely bleached washing. "I'd better be going."

Deepti, thought Jane. That was the girl's name. Clearly the washerwoman expected Deepti to understand English. What would it take to get the girl to talk to her?

As the clock ticked toward the hour when Lady Cromwell would descend to the parlour, Jane hurried Grandison back to Luke. She found the stableboy grooming a fine chestnut mare. After seeing the lantern-bearer last night – her first clue – it was time she made a proper start on her ghost-hunt. How better to set about it than with someone who had lived here all his life?

"Morning, Luke."

"I'm to be honoured by a visit from a fine lady, am I? Well, some of us have work to do."

That wasn't a good start. He was probably still feeling sore.

"She's a beauty," Jane commented.

Luke grunted and started on the mane.

"Who rides her?"

"No one yet. Sir Charles bought her for breeding."

"Oh?"

"Aye, her sire was Eclipse. They say she's going to Master Cromwell so he can set up his own breeding stock."

So this was the famous birthday present.

"Who's Eclipse?"

His lip curled. "I would've thought even a rector's daughter from Steventon would've heard of him."

"Enlighten me," she said sourly.

"He's only the most famous horse ever, winner of eighteen races and piles of gold for his owner."

"So he's very good?"

"*Was* good. He died in February. That sent the value of his foals sky-high as there won't be any more of them. Sir Charles didn't expect that when he bought Arachne here."

The name had something to do with spiders, didn't it? The Greek Arachne challenged the goddess Athena to a weaving match and was turned into a spider for her daring. Jane tried not to shiver. "Why Arachne?"

"'Cause of the spider. Come and see." He gave her the kind of grin her brothers did before doing something unspeakable, like dropping one down her neck.

"I'm not keen on spiders." She said it calmly, but she had been known to run SCREAMING when she found one in her washing basin. (They appeared there with alarming frequency, which she thought was also due to her brothers.)

Luke gave her a scornful look.

"Fear of spiders is quite rational!" she protested, though she suspected that she might carry it to excess. She couldn't help it.

"If you say so, Miss." She hesitated. "Come on: I dare you." His eyes were sparkling.

No Austen turned down a dare.

Jane ventured in, keeping her eyes open for any large, hairy spiders who were very likely to make their home in such a comfortable stable now she thought about it.

"So brave, Miss, even though it's the size of a dinner plate and can bite you."

"You can see it?" Jane asked fearfully. "Where?"

Smirking, Luke passed her something. She yelped when she felt the feathery extensions but it was only a carrot top to feed the horse.

"There's the spider." He pointed to the mare.

There was a white blaze on the horse's forehead that radiated like a spider's web. Luke had just been teasing – that made him in her judgment a RASCAL and an HONORARY Austen.

"You could've just told me it wasn't real!" She threw the carrot at him.

"But it was more fun to watch you hop about as if you could avoid a spider that way. Don't you know they drop from the ceiling and wriggle down your back?"

"Urgh! You're horrid!"

"I know." He grinned at her.

Jane wasn't really annoyed with him; it was definitely something she would do to a sister or friend, just not about spiders.

"Does Master Cromwell like horses as much as his father does?" She wouldn't wish such a beautiful creature to go to a careless owner.

"No one can like horses as much as Sir Charles does," said Luke, taking up the grooming tools. "He spends most days out here with them. He trades his foals to improve his stock. I think he's after creating the perfect horse."

"Does such a thing exist?"

The mare snorted in Jane's face, as if to say, "Of course. You're looking at her."

"From what he said, Eclipse came close with just a few minor faults. But the daughter is promising to make up for her father's bad points."

"So she's the last of her kind?"

"Until she has foals herself, with a carefully selected mate. Maybe Romeo. Sir Charles is still deciding."

"It doesn't sound to me like Sir Charles wants to give her away."

"You could've knocked me over with a feather when they said that this horse was the birthday gift. I reckon Lady Cromwell tricked him into it." Luke dropped the comb into the bucket. "And I'll believe it when I see it."

"He sounded yesterday at tea like he was sticking to the plan."

"There's a difference between promising your right hand to someone and actually cutting it off, even for your own son," said Luke. "I'd better be getting on, Miss. Fine ladies might have time to chat, but I'll get a clip around the ear if I do."

Jane realized she'd got sidetracked. "Before I go, can I just ask you something?"

He gave her a wary look. "What would that be?"

"Have you ever heard any stories of a ghost haunting the Abbey?"

"That old tale, Miss?" He scuffed the ground with the toe of his boot.

"My brother said something, before I came. I just wondered if it was true." She kept quiet about the light she'd seen last night.

"There've been stories about the Abbey ghost as long as I remember." He shook his head at her sceptical expression. "You'd be a fool to take them lightly, Miss. He's called the Mad Monk and goes about in a grey habit, dripping blood and dragging a chain. If you meet him, then death follows soon after. None of us would be caught in the old Abbey after dark, not for anything."

His fear was infectious. "You've seen him?"

"Never seen him, never want to see him, Miss. I want to live to a grand old age." Luke gave Arachne a final brush through the forelock and picked up the bucket.

Jane considered herself dismissed. She gave Arachne a parting pat and scratched Grandison behind the ear, thinking how stories pick up a power of their own. If you believe you are going to die if you see the ghost, then doubtless you find a way of fulfilling your own prophecy. Jane was sure she was too level-headed to fall for such stuff.

Wasn't she?

Chapter 11

That evening at dinner, Sir Charles instructed Fitzwilliam to show off the miniature steam engine in the library.

"We must practise for the ball tonight," declared Sir Charles, piling his plate with little spicy meat parcels, which he called samosas. "It would be embarrassing to have everyone gathered and then it go off like a damp squib."

Fitzwilliam swallowed a mouthful of wine. "Would it not be better to invite the inventor of the machine to display it?"

"Ridiculous!" Sir Charles waved away the suggestion. "We can't have stable hands talking to noblemen."

"I'll show the guests, Pa," said Cromwell. "I'll get Luke to teach me how it works."

"Don't be silly, Wicky," said his mother. "You'll be dancing with the young ladies."

Cromwell narrowed his eyes at Fitzwilliam. "And Fitzwilliam won't?"

"He's not the birthday boy."

"He gets out of dancing with every giggling Miss from the district, and I have to dance every set: how is this fair?" Cromwell reached for the roast potatoes. "It's my birthday; I would've thought I could do what I liked!"

Jane cut her samosa into three parts and excavated a pea, taking heart that the pastry contained something she recognized. She took a cautious bite and the spices exploded in her mouth. She gulped some water.

"Too hot for you, Miss Jane?" chuckled Sir Charles.

"No, no, it's very, er, warming."

"Why can't I exhibit it?" persisted Cromwell.

"Because I asked Fitzwilliam to do so." Sir Charles rapped his knife hilt on the table when he saw his son open his mouth again. "It's settled, Cromwell. I have spoken. We'll try it out after dinner."

After the meal had finished, they assembled in the library. Jane was eager to see the miniature steam engine, even if Luke wasn't here to show it to them. The device was set out on a baize-covered table. It was a wooden box topped by a wheel about the size of a plate, a balance beam taken from a set of scales, and a little boiler.

"Make it work, Fitzwilliam," ordered Sir Charles.

The young man leaned over the instrument and examined the separate parts. He opened the door of a tiny furnace. "Remarkable. I've only ever seen a full-size version on display at an agricultural fair, but I think we'll need some water in this boiler section." He tapped a cylinder sitting on top of the heater. "The steam will run through this little pipe and the pressure in the pistons will turn the flywheel."

Jane came closer, eager to follow his explanation. "What fuel does it use?" she asked. It was no bigger than a spinning wheel.

"He's been using lamp oil." Fitzwilliam filled the boiler with water, then lit the fuel with a flame taken from one of the candles on the mantelpiece. He then stood back.

Lady Cromwell turned away in disgust. "Nothing's happening!"

"You have to wait until the water boils, ma'am," said Fitzwilliam. He felt the metal side of the boiler. "It's barely warm yet."

"If I want boiled water, I'll have Parks use a kettle. Jane, we'll return to the parlour."

Jane wanted to scream. Lady Cromwell was IMPOSSIBLE! "Yes, my lady."

"Oh come, come, Mother: you've hardly given it a decent chance! And I can see Miss Austen is desperate to see it work. Take a seat by the fire and I'll bring you a cherry brandy," said Cromwell, expertly steering his mother to a chair. He signalled to the hovering Parks.

That was the second occasion on which he'd rescued her in as many days, thought Jane.

Cromwell caught her looking and winked. Jane pointedly inspected the folds of her gown. She didn't want him thinking she liked him.

By the time Parks returned with the brandy, the engine was showing signs of stirring. The balance beam went up, then dropped down as the steam was released. The wheel spun faster and faster; puffs of escaped vapour filled the air. The machine hummed, wheel spokes blurring with the speed. Then a whistle sounded.

With a muttered oath, Fitzwilliam disconnected the wheel and opened the door to the furnace. Using his pocket handkerchief to protect his fingers, he moved the little oil heater out from under the boiler so the water would have a chance to cool down.

"Why on earth did you stop it?" asked Sir Charles.

"It appears our Luke is even cleverer than I thought. He attached a brass whistle to the exhaust pipe so that, if the pressure mounts too high, it will sound," said Fitzwilliam.

"Humph!" Sir Charles folded his arms and scowled. "It didn't last very long, did it? I was hoping for something more exciting."

Jane was to discover that he would get his wish sooner than anyone expected.

Chapter 12

J ane went to bed and dreamed of spinning wheels powered by steam engines. She woke up abruptly in a cold sweat. It was the middle of the night. The owl hooted in distant woods, but inside the house all was quiet. She lay for a moment, heart pounding, wondering what was wrong with her. Of course, on other nights when she had a disturbing dream, she always had her sister to turn to. Cassandra might snore a little, and had terrible cold feet for most of the year, but she was a comforting presence to chase away the night terrors.

Shivering, Jane got up and went to the window. Would she see the light again? It felt about the same time as last night. Her view didn't include the ruins. She needed to find a better window and keep watch. If all the servants were as scared of the ghost as Luke, none of them would ever investigate the night wanderer. She wasn't scared, was she?

WAS she?

Jane pondered her choices: she had retreated last night in a very un-Austen fashion, but this time she had already explored the Abbey by daylight and knew she wouldn't sleep unless she did find out more. The library lay at the far end of the main house and had windows overlooking the ruins. Pushing her bare feet into her boots, she slid her arms into a grey dressing gown, and wrapped a shawl around her shoulders for warmth. Lighting a candle, she tiptoed downstairs.

In the back of her mind, she could hear her mother scolding.

Young ladies do not go wandering at night. Young ladies do not poke their noses into other people's business. The problem with that kind of young lady was that she sounded a deadly bore to Jane.

As Jane approached the library, she heard the murmur of male voices. The candelabra were still lit on the mantelpiece though the rest of the library was in shadows. Wondering who could be up at this hour, Jane paused outside.

"He's such a disappointment to me," said Sir Charles. "Why can't he be more like you?"

"Sir?" The other voice belonged to Fitzwilliam. Peering through the crack by the hinges, Jane saw him perched awkwardly in the armchair facing Sir Charles. Fitzwilliam was nursing a glass of amber liquid but not sipping. Sir Charles, by contrast, was taking great swigs, then topping up the tumbler from a decanter on the table beside him.

"A celebration? That's a joke! It's more like a commiseration. He shows no interest in learning how to run the estate, precious little even in raising the horses; all he can talk about is travelling, and new ideas, and America of all places. Nothing good ever comes from that country, I can tell you."

Jane knew she shouldn't be listening – would be in trouble if she were caught – but she couldn't stop herself now she had started.

"I'm sure he'll settle down, sir, when he's ready," said Fitzwilliam, glancing desperately at the grandfather clock. It looked like he'd been listening to these complaints for many hours.

"What's wrong with this generation, Fitzwilliam?" Sir Charles waved his glass and the brandy sloshed. "You want to tear everything up and have no idea of what you want in its place!"

"I don't think Cromwell really wishes to give up his privileges, sir."

Sir Charles pointed an index finger at him. "You're right! He likes to talk of 'we the people', constitutions and rights, but he couldn't plough a field or even mend a pot if he had to live like one of the common men. I never see him go into a cottage, inspect a field, ask the village doctor who's ill, who's dying. No, he just rides around tipping his hat to pretty milkmaids and generally feeling he is a fine fellow."

"I'm sure there's more to him than that, sir."

"I've not seen it. And what about that business that had him sent down from Oxford? Releasing a greased pig during the chapel service! And why didn't you stop him?"

"It's hard to stop a greased pig, sir."

Jane bit her lip to prevent a giggle escaping. The image of all the students, choristers, and dons trying to grapple a pig was wonderfully absurd.

"Not the pig, you imbecile! My son!"

"I didn't know what he'd planned, sir."

"I sent you to Oxford to look after him."

Ah! So, Fitzwilliam had got the job that her brother had failed to obtain. Henry had had a lucky escape.

"I apologize once again, sir. I disappointed you." Poor Fitzwilliam: he was being blamed for failing at an impossible task.

"You have – but not as much as my son. If he had a tenth of your dedication to improving himself, I would be content."

The grandfather clock struck two.

"More brandy?" said Sir Charles.

"It's late, sir."

"Yes, I suppose it is. It's too late for Cromwell; his mother has spoiled him. Off to bed with you. We'll take a look at the bottom field tomorrow. I'm off to check on the horses before I turn in."

That meant they were coming her way!

Chapter 13

J ane quickly retreated into an alcove and hid her candle as Fitzwilliam headed to his chamber. Sir Charles followed, holding a four-branch candelabrum to light his way. She would be seen if he turned his head! Backing up, she found she had entered the servants' staircase. Breath held, she waited, hoping the master of the house wouldn't stoop to use this route. Sure enough, he strode past.

That was close – too close!

Remembering the ghost that had drawn her from her room, Jane decided she might as well not waste the opportunity. Sir Charles was going to the stables and everyone else was in bed; there still might be something to see outside. She headed downstairs.

Turning the key in the door leading to a yard at the side of the house, Jane crept out, cupping her hand over the candle. It guttered and danced until a breeze snuffed it out. She should've found a lantern. Still, if she waited for her eyes to adjust, she should be able to find her way by starlight. It was a clear night so there were thousands strewn across the sky.

Leaving the kitchen yard through an old archway, she carried on to the original parts of the Abbey. These were connected to the main house by a ragged stone wall, once a corridor that kept the monks dry as they passed from chapel to their lodgings. Beyond lay the ruins. In the middle of this tumbled-down place, Jane paused. There was something magical about being out of bed in a forbidden abbey when everyone else was asleep. She stood free under the heavens, just a girl, looking up at the stars, feeling at once very small and very powerful. Her fancy told her that she could pluck any star she chose from the sky and swallow it like the fiery samosa she had tried earlier. Burning in her chest, the fallen star could power her through the next day. She would be a creature of imagination and starlight.

A glimmer of light in one of the window arches of the chapel dragged her attention back to earth. The mysterious lantern bearer was here! What was he doing? Innocently enjoying the night like she was? Unlikely. But wait a moment! How could the light be so high up? There was no floor at the level of the windows. It had to be hovering in mid-air.

Jane darted forward, determined to get into the chapel enclosure before the light vanished, but when she stepped into the nave, there was no sign of the lantern. It had vanished. She rubbed her eyes. She had definitely seen it. It had been no dream.

The hair prickled on the back of her neck.

What was that to the right, behind the altar? Now the lantern was floating in the darkness beyond the fallen back wall of the chapel. Jane ran through the ruined Abbey, but once again, when she reached the spot where she should have a clear sight of the carrier, the light had vanished.

This was foolish. All she need do is call out.

But what if it were someone wicked? A thief, poacher, or vagabond? Or a ghost?

The glimmer again! Now high up, floating across the old cloister. Jane took a shuddering breath. The adventure that had started out as a delicious bit of snooping had turned into something far scarier. Lanterns did not float – not real ones.

Was it really a ghost that carried a death curse? It had been very easy to dismiss the idea in a busy inn yard in full daylight, but now...

Investigate, find the evidence, and then draw your conclusions, she told herself. *Don't disgrace the Austens!*

Jane picked up the skirts of her long nightdress and strode out of the east end of the chapel. She walked determinedly toward the light. Oh yes, they wouldn't escape her this time, not if she could help it.

One more step and Jane's right foot found no ground beneath it.

With a shriek, she tumbled down a stone shaft and landed on a pile of earth and mouldering leaves at the bottom, some eight feet below. Something clattered overhead and a wooden cover dropped back into place, shutting out the stars. A chain rattled, scraping on the planks, then silence.

Chapter 14

"Of all the foolish things you've done, Jane," she told herself, "this might top the list." She searched the walls frantically with her fingertips, trying to find a door or steps, but it was a solid box structure. What was it? A stone sepulchre? *No, no, Jane, stop it.* No coffin (thank goodness) or inscription had met her touch. It was far more likely to be a cellar like the one at the rectory, used for storing turnips or barrels of pickled herring. The only way in or out was through the wooden trapdoor at the top and, try as she might, she couldn't reach that. Shouting and tapping on the walls with a pebble brought no response.

Tired and desperate, Jane sat down on a slightly less damp pile of leaves and hugged her knees. Fear of spiders kept her from disturbing the heap of earth any more than she had to.

Don't think of spiders. DO NOT think of spiders.

Oh lord, she was thinking of them: big black legs, scuttling, crawling... She whimpered. She had to do something before panic struck.

"Look on the bright side." Her voice sounded thin in the darkness but she pressed on, pushing back the panic, inch by inch. "Your absence will be noticed by the time Lady Cromwell gets up at noon." Glumly, she thought the likelihood of the household caring about the movements of an unimportant guest any earlier was close to zero. "All you are facing is an uncomfortable few hours. That's all. And you've got an answer of sorts: surely it was a person and not a ghost who played this trick on you." Unless ghosts could move physical objects; she was hazy on the details of what ghosts were thought capable. "But you don't believe in them so dismiss that from your mind. No spectre is going to float in here and scare you to death." Was it? Jane pummelled her knees. She was so angry with herself for half-believing it had been a ghost.

"I refuse to be found as a pile of bones a century later; that just doesn't happen to an Austen. My family will make sure there is a proper search even if the Cromwells don't."

Maybe thinking about turning into a skeleton was not the best approach? *Think sensible thoughts.* She was a few hundred feet from help. When morning came, there were bound to be people up and about. She just had to wait and then shout loud enough to attract their attention.

Praying that rescue would come sooner rather than later, Jane tied the shawl more closely around her and tried to doze, propped up in one corner.

Sleep was beyond her. She supposed she was lucky that it was June so there was no chance of freezing to death, but the stone sapped all warmth from her limbs. Her toes were freezing. Another disquieting thought struck her. If – when – she was rescued, how was she going to explain why she ended up here? She was in her nightdress. Girls did not go roaming around at night improperly dressed. She tried out some of her explanations:

"I went looking for a ghost" – ridiculous!

"I fancied a breath of fresh air" – eccentric
  for a young lady.

"I sleepwalked" – a lie, but it had the advantage of being
  beyond her control so she was less likely to be blamed.

If the wrong person found her, and a report got back to Sir Charles, an abrupt journey back on the coach lay in her future tomorrow, no matter her excuse. Just like Henry. She would fail her family utterly and just confirm her mother in her low opinion of her. This was a disaster.

Chapter 15

D awn came early in midsummer. After a few hours, Jane could see grey cracks appearing around the wooden trapdoor. They brightened so that a little light fell on the earthen pile on which she sat. There were no unpleasant surprises now it was no longer completely dark – no prisoners chained to the wall, no caskets of ancient monks. There was a scrap of sacking sticking out of the heap.

"Turnips," Jane muttered, feeling vindicated.

Straining her ears, she waited for signs of human life. She could hear birds striking up a dawn chorus and distant clattering coming from the kitchens, but no one was near enough to hear her call. She tried combining shouts with her piercing whistle.

It would work – it had to! Jane Austen couldn't end up dead in a cellar a stone's throw from help.

Ten minutes after she'd whistled, a familiar scratching and barking erupted on the trapdoor above. Of course! She should've considered that her prayers might be answered this way. Grandison had found her!

BEST DOG EVER!

"Oh, you wonderful creature!" Jane called. "Get help, Grandison."

Sadly, he was not trained in such practical matters. He bounced around on the wooden lid and barked, wondering why Jane hadn't come out despite the fact he'd found her. She wasn't playing the game properly, his hysterical barks said.

An excruciating few minutes passed and then Jane heard someone say something to Grandison. She couldn't catch the words but that didn't matter: they were human, with hands to open doors, and arms to let down a rope.

"In here!" Jane shouted. She added a whistle for good measure, as this appeared to have carried all the way to the stables for the sharp-eared hound. "HELP!"

The door lifted, bathing Jane in what seemed blinding light after spending so long in the dark.

"Miss?"

Jane shaded her eyes. Deepti was peering down at her, her long black plaits dangling over the hole. Her father joined her, as did Grandison: all three an inquisitive audience to her predicament.

"I fell in last night," Jane said, deciding that accusations of ghostly misdeeds would not be helpful.

"I'll get a rope," said Arjun, going straight to the essentials of the situation.

While he went off to find one, Deepti patted Grandison, trying to calm the excitable hound. "Are you hurt, Miss?" she asked.

"No. I had a soft landing, fortunately." Jane gestured to the earthen pile.

"How did you close the door?"

"I didn't. I think someone might've shut it. I heard chains and I thought they might be locking it."

Deepti frowned. "There are no chains. It wasn't locked. There was only a... how do you call it?" She made a gesture with her hands.

"A bolt?"

"Yes, a bolt – but that was open. And no padlock and chain."

"Then I must be mistaken." Jane knew that wasn't true. She'd heard what she'd heard, but this was not the moment to start babbling about ghosts.

Arjun returned with a stout rope, formed a loop at one end, and lowered it down. "Place that around your waist, Miss," he said. "I'll pull you up."

The rope went taut and slid up to under her arms but, by holding on, Arjun lifted Jane out with impressive ease. She found herself back on the grass and was tempted to fall on her knees in relief.

"Thank you so much." She gave Grandison an enthusiastic stroke to convey her gratitude. "And you, you clever dog!"

Arjun waved away her thanks. "Not at all. But the ruins are not a good place to wander. It is forbidden."

"I know that now." Getting her bearings, she noticed that father and daughter were both wearing unusual garments: loose black jacket and trousers, shocking garb for an English girl but somehow they looked perfectly decent on Deepti. On the ground nearby lay four short swords, long bone handles and slightly curved blades. They looked the kind a warrior might have at his belt for close-quarter fighting, like a sailor's cutlass. "I interrupted something?"

Deepti glanced at her father. "Only our morning exercise. But please, we'd prefer you not to tell Sir Charles we come here." They had chosen a spot where the Abbey walls sheltered them from the windows of the house. Jane realized that they too were, of course, flouting the ban.

"Your secret is safe with me." She coughed. "I'd... er... be grateful if you don't mention my unfortunate accident."

"No harm done so the master has no need to know," said Arjun, bowing. "Won't the maid who brings the hot water notice you are out of bed?"

"You make a very good point." Jane was tempted to copy his bow but decided on a curtsey instead. "I'll let you get back to whatever it was you were doing. Would you mind keeping Grandison for me? He's not allowed in the house and should return to the stable, but I can't take him there in my nightgown."

"We will." Arjun slipped his fingers through the dog's collar. "I'll take him back. But will he stay with us once you are gone?"

Jane fixed Grandison with her best firm stare. "Grandison, stay!"

He doggy-grinned at her.

She pointed at Arjun. "Biscuit!"

Now she was getting serious. Grandson sat and waited, drool spooling from his jaws. "Would you mind finding him a treat for obeying?" Jane asked.

"I'm sure I can find him something. He is a faithful dog, worthy of a biscuit." Arjun scratched Grandison under the chin.

Jane hurried away while the order still lodged in Grandison's head.

He was liable to forget when a new distraction came his way. Looking back to check all was well, Jane saw that Deepti had picked up two of the swords and began a... a what? A dance? Jane had seen a Highlander jig over crossed swords once, but this was closer to ballet. Deepti's father sat beside the dog, still holding his collar, and gave her instructions. Deepti swirled, dipped, and thrust, swords an extension of her arms. Good heavens: the girl was practising with weapons she clearly knew well and was skilled at using. This was a female accomplishment Jane had never met before – so much better than embroidering a screen. *How splendid!*

Questions had to wait. Jane scampered up the servants' stairs. She reached the top corridor without incident and dashed into her room. Footsteps alerted her to the arrival of her washing water so she kicked off her boots and leaped under the covers, trying not the think of the mud she must be tracking with her. Pulling the quilt up to her ears, she feigned sleep.

"Morning, Miss," said the maid, putting down the jug on the stand and opening the curtains, "Did you sleep well?"

"Good morning, Mary. Yes, like a log," lied Jane.

A Letter of Increasing Importance

Cassandra.

Dearest sister.

(In fact, <u>only</u>.

So also <u>least</u> dear.)

I send you affectionate greetings.

I have had a ghostly adventure.

This ended with fall down a hole.

Not a clever end for any self-respecting Austen.

However, Grandison saved me from being lost for ever.

An intriguing father and daughter, both Hindoos who sword dance, assisted.

We must ask them to the next entertainment at the Biggs's.

Steventon will never be the same once you see this new accomplishment.

But what about the ghost? you cry as you weep over my letter.

So sad — I appear to have run out of room and must save this.

I remain, as ever, your rescued but ever so slightly bruised spectre-hunting sister, Jane Austen.

Chapter 16

That afternoon, Lady Cromwell was persuaded to venture out as far as the gazebo in the rose garden. Temperatures had risen during the day, but it was pleasant in the shade and a breeze kept it from feeling stuffy. Climbing roses peeked through the lattice like little pink faces at the theatre, waiting for an entertaining show. That made Jane and Lady Cromwell the actors on the stage. Jane feared the rose-audience would drop their petals in disappointment. There was nothing to see here but two females in summer dresses (Jane in her newly promoted second-best) engaged in the unobjectionable female talent of sewing. What Jane would give for a more flamboyant accomplishment, like sword dancing! That would make the families around Steventon sit up at the next evening party. *Miss Bagnell will entertain us with an extract from Handel's oratorio; Miss Biggs will sing a ballad; Miss Jane Austen will show us her skill with blades, displaying a move that can take down a tiger and fillet a fish in one smooth slice.* Jane smiled: the old biddies would be up in arms – and her family ostracized, prospects for marriage ruined… Perhaps it was a skill that better stay out of the Austen family repertoire.

Having rewound Lady Cromwell's silks (*Jane 1, Muffin 1* – something would have to be done about that cat), Jane was allowed to sit and read. She'd chosen from the library a volume by her favourite poet, Cowper. He didn't require her full attention as she knew his verse so well; that left her a space to think about her night-time adventure. Ghosts once more retreated in the sunshine. So, who had closed the lid on her? She had to allow the possibility that it had been left propped open by some neglectful servant and her fall had dislodged it. Deepti had said it wasn't locked so it could merely have dropped into its usual place. Perhaps the bolt had rattled and the tale of the Mad Monk had encouraged her to think of it as chains? She would be ashamed to find herself so gullible.

But what about the lantern-bearer? How had it appeared as if the light were floating far above the ground?

I refuse to believe in ghosts, thought Jane. She resolved to go and take a closer inspection of the ruins when Lady Cromwell could spare her. She would take more care this time; she had no wish to fall into another trap for the unwary.

The dullness of the afternoon was much lightened when Fitzwilliam approached the bower. He looked worried, Jane noticed, paler than yesterday. Something had upset him.

"Ah, Fitzwilliam, have you finished it?" asked Lady Cromwell, laying aside her needle.

"Almost, my lady. I only have the last century to cover." He hesitantly passed her a large bound notebook.

The lady took it with delight and flicked through. "This is splendid. Wicky will love his present. Fitzwilliam, you really are so useful."

Jane was dying for someone to say what was going on. If she had been Grandison, she would've whined and placed a paw on Lady Cromwell's lap.

"I'm not sure you are going to keep to that opinion, my lady," Fitzwilliam said glumly.

"Oh?" The lady put the book down.

"I found some land deeds from the seventeenth century this morning. Your ancestors had a stormy time during the Civil War. They were fortunate that they were able to keep the estate."

"How so? I'm afraid I don't understand all that historical stuff." The lady fluttered her hands as if the past was like a complex mathematical problem.

"When king and Parliament fought, the men in the family found themselves on opposing sides. I think it was possibly on the orders of

Lord Withers, so he had a foot in both camps and someone of his blood would emerge on the winning side."

"What were they fighting about?" asked the lady, brow wrinkling.

"The Civil War, ma'am. Sir Charles is a distant relative of Oliver Cromwell, the man who became the Lord Protector when they beheaded Charles I."

Jane gauged that this was news to the lady. What had Lady Cromwell done with her time when she was in the schoolroom? Any Austen would be ashamed to be so ignorant of their history.

"Beheading a king – that's not very British!" said the lady.

"It was, in the seventeenth century at least," countered Fitzwilliam. "Perhaps I should return to your ancestor?"

"Please do."

"Lord Withers transferred some of the land, the Abbey and estate, to his eldest daughter and she kept aloof from politics. As control swapped between king and Parliament, she retained the land around the Abbey, as she was judged a neutral party by both sides. However, when the dust settled, she refused to pass it back to her oldest male relative as had been her father's plan. She wanted to take it as a substantial dowry to her husband-to-be."

Jane could hardly blame her. Women rarely got to own anything, as owning something gave them power.

Some of this must have been familiar to Lady Cromwell, as her face brightened. "Is that Lady Sophia, my namesake? My father said, when he had no sons, he hoped I would grow up as wily as her."

"Indeed."

Jane admired the way Fitzwilliam avoided having to give an opinion on the outcome of Lady Cromwell's development.

"I know the rest of that story," said the lady, taking the book back into her lap. "She is famous in our family – cursed by the Withers branch and praised by mine. The existing Lord Withers carries it so far to say he won't talk to any lady called Sophia." She giggled. "That is a relief, I can tell you, because he never misses an opportunity to let anyone know that the Abbey should have come to his forebears; all he has is a name, a few minor houses, and a modest fortune from investments. From trade, would you believe it?" She sniffed at the disgrace.

Fitzwilliam gave her a pained smile. "Then it is better, perhaps, that he does not have sight of the original documents transferring the land. I'm not a legal expert but I would say there was some… ambiguity about the terms."

"Where?"

"I've made a note. There's a bookmark in the place."

The lady opened the tome. "I can't understand this. What is it? Latin?"

"It's legal language, my lady. I think it says, in effect, that the Abbey and lands remain with your branch of the family until such time as there is no male heir. I understand that the original Lady Sophia stood resolute and negotiated this compromise with her father. As part of the arrangement, her husband agreed to adopt the family name and he became Withers-Crompton."

"My maiden name," the lady said happily, not picking up on the signals that Fitzwilliam was working up to an unpleasant surprise.

"Yes. She fulfilled the terms by giving birth to a male heir within a year of the marriage. The Withers-Cromptons got to keep the house as a result. Each generation that followed produced sons. It is only in your father's day that this clause was not fulfilled, as he had only daughters, but by then the condition had been forgotten by all parties to the arrangement. And as your son was born before your father's death, it could be argued that a male heir existed, even if it had skipped a generation. A final ruling would, however, have to be decided in court. I'm certainly not competent to say which way it would go."

Lady Cromwell shut the book with a snap. "On second thoughts, I think you should end your history of the Abbey at Henry VIII. Wicky will enjoy reading about monks and battles far more than dusty documents that no one remembers."

Fitzwilliam bowed. "As you wish, ma'am."

Hesitating, she gave him a worried look. "Who else knows this?"

"Just us, my lady. If the present Lord Withers had known, he would've raised this when your father died."

"You've not told Sir Charles?"

Fitzwilliam had the expression of one who had just bitten into a lemon. "Would you like me to?"

"No!" In her distress, the lady knocked her embroidery to the floor. Jane scooped it up, shook the dust off, and passed it back. Lady Cromwell was recalled to the fact that this conversation had a witness. "Jane, you will keep anything you see and hear here a secret, I trust? You aren't a tattletale?"

"No, ma'am."

OH, BLAST! thought Jane, mentally underlining it several times. She now had a delicious, damaging secret and she could do nothing with it, except one day write about it at a slant. She made a mental note to jot down the details later.

The lady turned back to Fitzwilliam. "And the documents you read, where are they?"

"Among the family papers, my lady, bound together with other deeds and wills. They are all kept in the library. I imagine a copy was also lodged at Doctors' Commons in London with the lawyer for the family."

"But it has been forgotten?"

"So it seems."

"So we can forget it exists then?"

Fitzwilliam looked uneasy. "I…"

The lady's vapid gaze took on a surprising steely cast. "Fitzwilliam, do you wish to return to Oxford and continue your studies?"

"Of course, my lady."

"Then I will ensure that you do – after the summer."

"Thank you, my lady."

"No good will come of stirring up old disputes. Wicky is a male heir. The house will go to him. Take this with you and make the necessary changes." She held out the book. "Get rid of the unnecessary parts."

Fitzwilliam bowed his head and withdrew.

"How anyone can read that legal language, I don't know," the lady said in a flustered tone. "Two lawyers, three opinions, my father always said. Nothing is clear and straightforward."

Jane opted for her standard answer. "Yes, my lady."

"You didn't see the clause, did you, Jane?"

"No, my lady."

"It was very garbled – could well have meant the opposite."

"Of course, my lady."

Because if it meant what Fitzwilliam thought, the Cromwells were in

ILLEGAL occupation of the house and grounds, Jane realized. The estate should have reverted to Lord Withers and not come to Lady Cromwell. Her heir would inherit NOTHING if it got out.

Jane shivered, a sensation her mother said was like someone treading on your grave. Such knowledge might be very dangerous. Time to make herself very, very insignificant. She summoned up a vague expression.

"I fear all that went quite over my head, my lady."

"And mine." The lady smiled. "Read a poem, Jane. Let's drive off all this silly talk with something from your book. What are you reading?"

"Cowper, my lady."

"Oh, well, he'll have to do. Pick a favourite – the one about growing cucumbers." The lady took up her sewing and tried to continue her day as if nothing earth-shattering had just happened, but from the fine trembles in her hand, Jane knew Lady Cromwell had sense enough to be shaken. That was one birthday gift the lady would wish she had never commissioned.

Chapter 17

Lady Cromwell only lasted another half-hour in the garden before declaring she was fatigued and needed to lie down in a cool room. She said it was the heat, but Jane suspected it was the shock of Fitzwilliam's revelation that had knocked her for six. Jane followed her inside, carrying the basket of silks with the embroidery balanced on top.

"If Sir Charles asks, I'll not come down until the guests arrive, Parks," Lady Cromwell said feebly as her lady's maid assisted her up the stairs.

"Yes, my lady," said the butler.

"When are the first guests expected?"

"Viscountess Felix and party intend to be here for dinner, which we are holding back to seven on Sir Charles's orders."

"Then I'll have a tray in my room – a little fresh lemonade with ice from the icehouse would set me up."

"I'll see to it, my lady."

She paused on the third stair. "And perhaps a cake or two?"

"Naturally, my lady."

There was another hesitation in the landing halfway up. "And I could possibly manage a few almond biscuits."

"At once, ma'am."

As the lady wilted upstairs, Jane considered herself dismissed until dinnertime. She was learning that Lady Cromwell responded to distress by eating. Jane had felt the same urge herself when upset, but there was no question what Mama would do if she caught Jane begging treats from the cook as a remedy for megrims. Sugar was expensive. She could hear her mother now. *The answer for low spirits is to show charity to the poor. Here, Jane, deliver this to a needy parishioner and then tell me your life is so hard.*

Jane admired her mother's forthrightness even if it did spoil a good sulk.

Leaving the basket and embroidery in the plum parlour, Jane gleefully contemplated her free afternoon. What to do first? Inspect the ruins? Check on Grandison?

Deciding her responsibilities as a pet owner could not wait, Jane went to the stables. Beyond the ha-ha, the nearest field was transforming into a fairground for the tenants' party the following day: workmen erected long tables, set up benches, strung multicoloured flags from bushes and trees. Archery butts stood ready at a safe distance from the maypole and cook tents. A travelling fair had made camp by the river, their painted wagons bringing a splash of colour to a green corner. Jane could see acrobats tumbling and standing on each other's shoulders as they ran through their routines. Oh, this was going to be splendid! Cromwell, for all his faults, had an excellent taste in parties. Jane thought she spotted Sir Charles and Cromwell among the men. They appeared to be discussing the best place for a wrestling ring as four labourers hovered with corner posts, shifting this way and that to find the flattest ground.

The stables were unusually quiet. Most of the stable hands were setting up for the party. That left Luke alone to unsaddle and walk Romeo until the horse had cooled from his afternoon ride. At the far end of the yard, an old groom washed the cobbles, limping to and fro each time he filled the bucket at the pump.

"Good day," Jane called.

Grandison trotted out from some hidden corner and woofed.

"Miss," said Luke. He was too busy to stop; his hands were full with the spirited stallion who was bucking and prancing near the mounting block. Jane watched as the boy gently worked the fidgets out of the horse. Jane kept her distance. Romeo looked overheated from his exercise, sides streaked with sweat. Sir Charles must've put him through his paces not long before.

When Luke judged the moment was right, he led the horse into his stable and Romeo stopped pulling on the halter, tension in his shoulders and flanks relaxing. He was pleased to be home. Jane could understand why. It was cooler in here, windows open high up to allow for natural ventilation. Sir Charles's horses had the very best of modern arrangements for their comfort.

"Romeo looks hot." She felt in her pocket for a sugar lump, taken from the tea tray for just this purpose. She held it flat on her hand and Romeo delicately lipped it from her palm.

Luke nodded. "Aye, that he is, but he's used to it. Sir Charles got him when he was abroad. He said Romeo's home is much hotter than ours and that he can stand being ridden hard even at noon in high summer in England."

"With a name like Romeo, he sounds like he comes from Italy and their summers are far warmer than ours."

"Miss?"

"Romeo is a character in a play by Shakespeare – one set in Verona in Italy. You've heard of Shakespeare?"

He paused in a sweep of his cloth down the horse's neck. "I'm not an idiot, Miss."

Jane realized she'd offended him again. "I apologize. Of course, you have."

"I've seen travelling players. They were grand folk, Miss! They did *Henry V* at the inn yard in Stratfield Turgis last year."

Jane had a third item to add to her list of things Luke liked:

1. *Horses*

2. *Dogs*

And now

3. *Plays.*

"Were they any good?" Jane loved the theatre but rarely got to see a play unless performed by family and friends. Mama didn't hold with going to shows in inn yards.

He shrugged. "There were lots of battles and shouting."

"Oh."

He grinned. "I enjoyed it."

They moved on to Arachne. The mare gave a snort and stamped her foot in greeting. Jane reached for a second sugar lump.

"I'm afraid, Miss, I lost Grandison for a time this morning," said Luke, putting fresh water in the mare's bucket.

"Oh?" Jane thought that was nice and vague.

"We were having breakfast out in the yard, Grandison and me, and then he shot off! I was frantic, as you might imagine, but I couldn't follow him; Mr Scroop was watching. I was worried I'd have to tell you I'd lost him, but then, blow me down, if Arjun, that Indian cook belonging to Sir Charles, didn't bring Grandison back an hour later!"

"Then there was no harm done?"

"Not that I've heard." Luke's tone suggested that he didn't put it past Grandison to have raided the hen coop or stolen the cook's sausages and his misdemeanour was only waiting to be revealed.

It was not fair for her dog to have an unearned reputation for disobedience. Jane weighed up telling Luke the truth. There was an advantage to taking him into her confidence: he'd lived here all his life so might know more about the ruins than she did. She decided to trust him, this honorary Austen.

"There was a reason that Grandison ran away," she began.

"Yes, Miss?" Luke took a pitchfork and began clearing out the old straw. First checking for spiders – there were none – Jane climbed up on the loose box partition to keep out of the way.

"I got stuck – down a hole in the ruins."

"Blimey, Miss. You shouldn't have been in there. What if you'd seen the Mad Monk!"

"I didn't." *At least, not definitely.*

Luke shook his head at her attitude. "Sir Charles has roped off that area. How did you get rescued?"

"Grandison heard my whistle. He got me help." She left out the night-time ramble and the scary hours before her rescue. She didn't need to tell Luke everything.

"Then there's more going on in that head than first appears," said

Luke, pausing to pat the attentive dog. "How did you manage to fall in?"

"Do you know the hole I mean?"

"There are several, but they've always been locked down when I've visited."

"I thought you said the ruins were forbidden?"

"They haven't always been out of bounds – just recently. Anyway, I only go there in daylight, 'cause of the monk, but I've rattled a few padlocks out of curiosity. What's it like down there?"

Jane hugged herself while maintaining her balance on the fence. "Cold. Full of mouldy leaves."

"No treasures or old bones?"

"Not that I could see."

"I suppose that was too much to hope. They'd've been cleared out long ago if they ever existed."

"I think the one I fell down was a cellar for the monastery. If there are bones and such, they'll be in the crypt under the chapel, so don't give up hope." Jane didn't want to strip Luke of his romantic ideas about the Abbey, and who knew? Maybe there were still secrets to be discovered under those walls? "If I have an adventure, I'm the sort who will end up finding a sack of potatoes. You might be the kind who finds a pot of gold."

"I doubt it, Miss." He paused and leaned on his pitchfork. "Life hasn't been so generous to me so far."

Chapter 18

Luke climbed the ladder to begin the process of forking down fresh straw. "Mind yourself!"

Jane sneezed as straw flew. "I'd better go!" she called up. "Thank you for looking after Grandison."

Luke wiped his nose on his sleeve, the dust getting to him too. "He's no trouble, Miss."

"I'll take him for a walk."

"Right you are."

Jane clipped the leash on to the dog. He trotted happily beside her, glancing up occasionally to see if her hand had filled miraculously with sugar lumps, but he was out of luck.

"Grandison, we are going to inspect the ruins again," Jane told him. "I need you to behave – that means you must not attract attention to us as we are trespassing, and you are to tell me if you find anything suspicious."

The dog gazed at her in adoration. *Oh well. He might turn up something despite himself.*

The ruins had no other trespassers that afternoon. With a feast to prepare, it was all hands on deck in the kitchens. Even the gardeners were absent, cutting greenery for the garlands and tidying the flowerbeds nearest the front of the house. As picturesque ruins were the height of fashion in landscaping, the tradition of having an outdoor summer ballroom on the lawn with the ruins as a backdrop was being revived and the Abbey was to be illuminated by a hundred lanterns. That was a task for Saturday, as Cromwell's tenants' party was taking up all the servants' time today. For the moment then, Jane was alone.

Letting Grandison off the leash to have a sniff, Jane retraced her steps. The trapdoor to the cellar was now padlocked shut. She wondered if Arjun had done that. It meant, though, that she couldn't lift up the lid and see how much pressure it took to make it drop down. When Arjun had opened the trapdoor to let her out, she remembered that it hadn't swung all the way back but stood at ninety degrees to the ground, movement restricted by its old hinges. It was plausible it had fallen under its own power – a puff of wind or just the vibration of her fall could have done it.

But why had the door been open in the first place? Had the lamp-bearer realized that he was being followed? Had he gone ahead and laid a trap? But why? To spite her? Or did he have something to hide? Had he been lucky to find the padlock missing or had he a key? That would narrow the field of suspects, as only a select few would be a key-bearer. Jane searched the ruins but could see nothing out of place, nothing taken, and nothing added. She did come across three more wooden doors, two more in the ground and one in a wall. All were locked and showed no recent signs of disturbance.

If the person (Jane refused to allow the idea of a ghost back into her deductions) had something to hide, then he had probably achieved his goal and moved on.

But what about the floating lantern?

Jane tried to remember where she had been standing when she'd seen it. In the nave of the chapel? She returned to take up position roughly where she thought she'd been and looked up in the direction of the light.

Oh, you foolish, FOOLISH girl! Why had she not thought of this possibility before? In the old windows of the chapel, workmen had erected mirror reflectors to hold candles for the illuminations. She hadn't seen a floating lantern; she'd seen a reflected one!

Chapter 19

One mystery solved, Jane wondered if that would be enough to earn her the half-crown from Henry. *No*, she decided. She had only solved the mystery of the optical illusion; he would argue the source of the light could still be the ghost. She was the one who had added the detail of it floating above the ground and scared herself silly.

Jane heard a whistle behind her and Grandison bounded over to Fitzwilliam. His enthusiasm was rewarded as the young man threw the cricket ball for him to fetch.

"I saw you from the library," Fitzwilliam said to explain his arrival. "You do remember that it is strictly forbidden to wander here without a guide?"

Jane had an inspiration. "I don't suppose you would be qualified to show me around?"

"I… I suppose I am. All right, I will satisfy your curiosity this once. But tell me: what are you doing here? Looking for your ghost?" His eyes were amused even when his tone remained quite sober.

He was nearer the truth than he knew. "No, sir. I don't believe in ghosts. I just like stories about them." She folded her arms, chin tilted in challenge. "Creating your history for Cromwell, you must have come across the tales. Why did you say there were none? Luke has since told me about the Mad Monk."

Grandison dropped the ball at Fitzwilliam's feet. Jane knew from

84

experience there would be no end to this game as far as the dog was concerned.

"That old chestnut! I can't cure the servants of their terror of that tale – Abbot Roderick, entombed alive in the crypt by a knight from the Withers clan in the thirteenth century, now walking by night to scare trespassers to death. I could have spouted that nonsense, I suppose." Fitzwilliam didn't look the least repentant. "But I thought then that you might be one of those impressionable novel-reading girls who see a ghoul or a wicked baron around every corner. Overheated imaginations should not be encouraged."

Jane couldn't let that pass without argument. Every Austen would fight to the death to defend fiction. "You don't like novels?"

His lips curved upward at her tone of outrage. "I like them well enough, as long as they keep their stories to what is possible in real life."

"We don't always want to read about everyday things – and that silly stuff is so much fun to parody."

He gave her a shrewd glance. "I dare say it is. Just don't put me in it, please, if you turn your pen to such things. I wouldn't like to read your portrait of me, not after today."

"Today?" Jane wondered how he had guessed about her writing. Had he seen her make notes? Or had he been the one to open the door to her room that first day? Her writings had been out for all to see before she thought to conceal them.

Having successfully fetched, Grandison dropped the ball at Fitzwilliam's feet. The young man threw it with an angry cast that had it sailing beyond the chapel walls. "You must think very poorly of me."

"I have no thoughts on the subject." That she could tell him, she added silently.

"But you must. There is a busy mind behind those hazel eyes of yours, Miss Austen. Lady Cromwell is a fool if she thinks you were not paying attention." They both looked expectantly to the archway through which the ball had sailed. Grandison had not yet returned. "Do you think he's lost it?"

"Or he's become distracted. Shall we go look for him?"

Fitzwilliam offered his arm and they set off in pursuit. Jane felt a little thrill of pleasure to be treated so well. She sensed, though, there was a reason for his appearance in the ruins to seek her out. He would tell her in his own time.

It didn't take long.

"I confess I am in a bind and I have to talk to someone about it or run mad," said Fitzwilliam. "You understand what I might've found in my research?"

"I believe so."

"It puts me in delicate situation. Is it my duty to mention it to Lord Withers when he comes for the ball?"

Jane grimaced. "So Lord Withers is coming here?"

"Yes, with his two sons – you can't miss them: both are built like haystacks."

Jane had an intriguing vision of two hayricks in evening dress dancing with society ladies. She was definitely going to have to spy on the ball.

"What do you think I should do, Miss Austen?"

"Me?" Jane was astonished to be consulted on so weighty a matter.

"You are a sensible girl, not biased by family ties. I would value your opinion."

Jane gulped. It was easier to be a wry observer than have to make decisions of such importance. "You've grown up here with the family?"

"Yes."

"And you're friends with Cromwell?"

"Yes – no." Fitzwilliam sighed. "Yes, we were friends as children. I'm not sure we like each other anymore."

"But you think the document is genuine?"

"I'm afraid so. Of course, it might merely end up with half the family fortune going on fighting it in the courts, only to return to the same arrangement as now."

"And the result of that would be everyone being worse off, especially you, as you would no longer be welcome here?"

He nodded. "And my father would almost certainly lose his position. So, should I speak out?"

Jane was a clergyman's daughter. Her father always preached that truth was preferable to lies, and that there was a sin of omission, too.

"Would you be in trouble if it came out another way and you were shown to have known all along?"

"I'm not sure. Lord Withers would certainly become my enemy and he is a man of influence. His sons would probably take their fists to me – that's how they prefer to settle disputes." He rubbed his jaw as if remembering an earlier disagreement.

"And if you arrive before St Peter at the pearly gates, what would you wish you'd done?"

"It's fairly simple when you put it like that."

Jane shook her head. "I don't think it is simple. The law is unfair to the female children. There is nothing worse than being raised in wealth and having it all taken away merely because you weren't born a boy. You might be guilty of reviving a past injustice."

"You may be correct, Miss Austen. I'll think upon it."

"If you decide to reveal what you've found, please give me due warning."

In a brotherly gesture, he patted her hand where it rested on his elbow. "Why? So you can take cover?"

So she could get out her notebook and find a front row seat. "Something like that."

Her smile had Fitzwilliam shaking his head again. "Dangerous," he muttered. "I was right about you."

They found Grandison had abandoned the ball for the delight of chasing rabbits. Jane clipped the leash back in place, bade farewell to Fitzwilliam, and towed her dog back to the stables.

It was a painful dilemma Fitzwilliam faced, she thought as she returned to the house. She hoped he found his answer soon.

A Letter of Marginal Importance

In haste I write another quick note, dearest Cassandra.

Now prepare yourself to be shocked!

Have you ever been burdened with a secret you cannot tell, even to your beloved sister?

Even now I struggle with such knowledge as would turn your hair white!

Really, it has nothing to do with a ghost or ghoul.

I think Hampshire will be shaken to the core if this gets out!

Though, sadly, I have been sworn to secrecy and must keep my vow.

An Austen does not break her word,

No hint will escape my lips as to what it is about.

Cassandra, you will have to look hard to share my secret with me.

Ever yours, Jane.

Chapter 20

For dinner with Viscountess Felix, Jane shook out her best gown. It wasn't much by London standards, but it passed muster in Hampshire. The gown had been copied from a print in a ladies' magazine: a cream cotton petticoat overlaid with a gauze skirt of the same colour. Jane had embroidered this, choosing honeysuckle as her theme, adorning the hem with green stems and pink flowers. It had taken hours that she would have much preferred to devote to writing, but a girl had to sacrifice much for fashion.

Pulling the gown over her chemise, Jane hit upon a snag. At home, her sister or mother was always on hand to help fasten the back. Try as she might, she could not reach. Unlike the acrobats she had seen earlier, she could not bend her arms behind her. She would have to ring for a servant, but the chance of getting one to answer her call with important visitors in the house was low.

Jane rang and waited.

And waited.

By her guess, the dinner hour was almost upon her. This was so frustrating!

An Austen did not let the little matter of buttons stand between her and what might be the best meal she would ever eat. She slipped into the corridor and knocked on the door a little further on.

The door opened a crack and Deepti looked out. "Miss?"

"Would you mind?" Jane turned around to show her the gaping back of the dress.

The door opened fully. Deepti's room smelled of sandalwood and spices, as if they had packaged up a little of their native breeze and released it in their room so they could "go home" each night.

"Come in, Miss. I'm alone," said Deepti, moving to let her pass.

Rabidly curious though she was, she tried to respect the family's privacy by keeping her eyes to the carpet. Deepti swiftly buttoned the material and smoothed it down.

"Thank you," Jane said.

"Would you like me to do your hair?" asked Deepti.

Jane's hand flew to her bun, which she thought she had secured neatly with pink and green ribbons.

"It is a little..." Deepti revolved her hand, suggesting all sorts of ragged possibilities at the back.

"Would you?"

"Please, sit." Deepti gestured to a stool at the foot of her bed.

The invitation to linger given, Jane allowed herself to raise her eyes. A rainbow of robes hung on pegs along one wall. A door was open, leading to a second room with a table and bed – a family room and Arjun's bedchamber, she guessed. Once seated, Jane felt swift fingers release and rearrange her hair. "I was really grateful that you rescued me this morning," she said.

"We were pleased to help."

A ribbon fluttered before her eyes and was then whisked away. Whatever Deepti was doing, it was far more complicated than the bow Jane had tied earlier.

"Do you mind me asking what exercise you were doing? It looked very exciting."

Deepti tugged and twisted hair with ribbon. "It is based on the *mardani khel* from my people." She spelled the word for Jane on her request. "Weapon dance. We are Maratha, from the hills. Father is one of our best warriors. When he came to India, Sir Charles hired him as his protector and to guard his possessions on the journey home."

"So he's not a cook?"

Deepti laughed wryly. "He is now. Sir Charles has no more use for his warrior skills. That was not his promise when we left Madras." She paused, then her true feelings burst out. "Sir Charles breaks his promises very easily."

Jane was conscious of the time running away from her. It was almost worth making a late entrance to get the rest of the story. "And now your father teaches you?"

"Yes."

"A girl?"

"Yes. Why? Is that odd?"

"It is here."

"In the royal courts in my land, it is sometimes necessary for women to fight. The princesses live separate from the men in houses called zenanas."

"Zenanas?"

"Enclosed spaces. I believe you call them 'harems' in your literature."

Jane had heard that word in the tales of *Arabian Nights*. She had forgotten that much of Persian culture had travelled to India with the Mughal Empire. "Oh yes!"

"The royal ladies are sometimes protected by female guards. When we go back, my father has promised I can be a bodyguard to a princess. He does not break his promises."

So it wasn't just a female accomplishment but a profession! Jane thought that just too magnificent for words.

Deepti patted Jane's shoulder. "Finished."

There was no mirror to see the back of her head so Jane gingerly felt what had been done. The ribbons now wound between her curls.

Deepti cocked her head to one side. "It looks very becoming." When Jane laughed, she frowned. "Did I use the wrong word?"

"No! It is just that I have never been made 'becoming' before. I have been 'passable' at most."

"Miss?"

"I have a very pretty older sister. Believe me, it is a trial to my vanity."

"I did not say you were beautiful."

"And I thank you for your honesty. I would not have believed you if you had raised my attractions above 'becoming'."

"Is she very beautiful, your sister?" Deepti sounded wistful. More for the sister than the beauty part, Jane guessed.

"Do you know, I'm not sure – and it doesn't matter to me. She's my best friend in all the world. I'd better run. Thank you for coming to my rescue – again!" Jane gave her a wave as she hurried out and down the stairs.

She met Parks in the hall as he directed footmen on the disposal of various items of luggage.

"Parks," Jane whispered. "Am I late?"

He smiled down at her. "Just a little. Sir Charles and Viscountess Felix's party are already inside. If I may suggest, you could enter the parlour from the morning room. There is a Chinese screen disguising the door and it would be as if you had always been there."

"You are a gem among butlers – thank you!" said Jane, picking up her skirts to make the diversion.

"If I might add, Miss, your hair is very –"

"Becoming! I know!"

Chapter 21

Jane slipped into the darkened morning room, which so far she had never seen used, possibly because the lady of the house did not bother with mornings. The voices in the parlour could be heard through the adjoining wall. Turning the knob on the door, she sidled into the room, protected, as Parks had promised, by the screen. The only creature to notice her late arrival was Muffin. The cat hissed in protest as Jane tipped her off a stool. Muffin tried to leap back on Jane's lap, but Jane was not risking her embroidered gauze on the cat's claws. She shooed her away so the cat sat down, shot up a leg, and washed her nether quarters in disgust.

Jane 2, Muffin 1, thought Jane.

"Lady Felix, how is the harvest shaping up on your estates?" boomed Sir Charles, walking further into the room into Jane's view. He took two drinks from a tray. It was strange to see him in awe of another person – a viscountess no less! The first Jane had ever met.

Viscountess Felix moved into sight to take the offered drink. She was a tall stick of a woman with a heaped-up topknot of iron-grey hair, who marched like a general reviewing his troops. "A fair harvest on my southern estates, Sir Charles. My stewards in the north and in Ireland are less happy. We need a decent run of good weather to rescue those plantings."

"Indeed we do." Sir Charles wanted to sound as if he knew what it

93

was like to struggle with a countrywide crop-growing problem rather than his own home farm on land he could see from his windows.

"Sophia!" said Viscountess Felix as the hostess made a late entry dressed in a stunning blue silk gown. "You look well. You'll remember my daughter, Annette?" She introduced a girl who looked perhaps twenty-four or five. Dark-haired and rake-thin like her mother, she would never be a belle of the ballroom. Jane liked her the better for it, as well as her air of self-possession as she curtsied to Lady Cromwell.

"Ma'am."

"Miss Felix, how you've grown since we last met," trilled Lady Cromwell.

"I hope not, for we met last month at the Carlton House ball," said Annette Felix.

Oooh, thought Jane, that was the way to deliver a put-down. She had a new heroine.

"Oh really? I forgot," fluttered Lady Cromwell.

"One meets so many people in London, one is sure to forget someone. I find I am eminently forgettable," Annette said with just a hint of a bite in her tone. "I understand, Sir Charles, you have a very good library here? Might I visit it during our stay?"

"Of course, my dear, though I hope you will remember that we are here to celebrate? No good being shut up indoors and missing the party!" Sir Charles's tone was overly hearty.

"I assure you I will be present for that," she said calmly. "But I am an early riser and I like to read in the mornings."

"Then I will make sure that the library is prepared for you. And… er…" Sir Charles's eyes fell on Jane, "Miss Austen here can show you the way and fetch anything you need for your comfort."

Attention now turned on her, Jane rose and curtsied. She was not required to speak, she knew that.

"That would be delightful." Annette gave her a curious look, trying to place Jane in the house pecking order.

"My wife's companion, daughter of the rector at Steventon," Sir Charles mumbled quickly, to reassure Viscountess Felix that he was not sending her daughter off in low company.

Viscountess Felix frowned. "Steventon?"

"An obscure parish, but they are good people. Connected to the Knights of Godmersham Park."

Jane grimaced. When she was little, her beloved third brother Neddy had been adopted by the childless Knights like a character in a fairy tale who came into unexpected riches. Ned was now destined for greater things, but she missed him.

"Father, don't say you started without me, the birthday boy!" Cromwell strode into the room, Fitzwilliam at his shoulder. "I'm so sorry we're late. There was a problem with the fair people and I went to smooth it over." He looked like he might have drunk ale with them too from the flush on his cheeks.

Sir Charles scowled. Jane could see he wanted to scold his son for choosing travellers over the nobility but daren't raise that suggestion in his guests' minds. "I trust all is now well?"

"Yes, yes, all settled for tomorrow. My lady." He kissed Viscountess Felix's hand. "Miss Felix." Annette kept her hands behind her back so he gave her a cautious bow.

That was interesting. He was genuinely impressed, or wary, of the lady. Annette was his elder by a few years and Jane could imagine her cutting through any twaddle Cromwell might spout in the ballroom.

"Now you're here, Cromwell, please see that Miss Felix has everything she requires," said Sir Charles. "You are taking her into dinner."

"It will be my pleasure. Miss Felix, would you care for something from the drinks tray?"

Jane watched the people in the room divide into their natural groups. Sir Charles, Lady Cromwell, and Viscountess Felix continued an awkward conversation, with the visitor's attention mostly straying to her daughter and Cromwell. Jane read the mother's expression as one of hope. In her mid-twenties, her daughter was considered almost "on the shelf", as she was not yet married; this explained their presence early at this gathering, as the viscountess must be wishing her daughter could make a match even at her advanced age. Sir Charles appeared to share that hope because he was giving the young people time alone. None of them would like the news that the inheritance could be in question. Fitzwilliam stood apart, knowing his presence would not be welcome in either grouping. His eyes met Jane's across the room and he gave her a rueful look. They were both judged too good to eat with the servants and too lowly to join in conversation with those with a title.

What a shame it was that wealth and large estates almost always went to a Lord or a Sir when a plain Mr was often more deserving, thought Jane.

Parks entered to summon all to the table. Fitzwilliam waited for the seniors to pass before offering Jane his arm.

"Miss Austen. Would you do me the honour?"

She smiled and rested her fingertips lightly on his forearm.

"Thank you, sir. I like your waistcoat." He was wearing a silk one with a delicate embroidery of cornflowers along the edge. "Do I detect Lady Cromwell's hand?"

"You do."

"She has great skill."

"Indeed. This was a gift last Christmas, to go with me to Oxford. I rarely have an occasion now on which to wear it." They were lagging a little behind the others. "Might I ask who did your hair? It is like something from a Greek statue."

"Is it really? I haven't been able to see it. Deepti did it for me."

"Then she is wasted in the laundry. I should mention it to Father."

Jane looked about her as if expecting the steward whom she was yet to meet to emerge. "Where is your father, if you don't mind me asking? I thought he would be here tonight."

A frown line appeared at the top of Fitzwilliam's nose. "He no longer attends public functions. He was seriously injured last year in a fall from a horse."

That explained why Sir Charles was taking Fitzwilliam about with him: not as a replacement son but as a trainee steward. It also gave a further twist to the difficulty Fitzwilliam was in over the inheritance: he had to protect his father too.

"I'm sorry. Is he recovering?"

"He is walking again – with two sticks – but Sir Charles has no patience with those who can't ride. I daresay Father will survive being deprived of an evening of bowing and scraping."

"But you don't want to be at Southmoor – you want to finish university?"

"I do but…" He shrugged, suggesting the impossibility of that plan. "I found I had a liking for studying law." He said this in a wistful tone.

Lady Cromwell knew her man well when she chose the bribe for his secrecy. "You don't wish to stay here?"

"I have to think ahead, Miss Austen. Cromwell won't want me around when he inherits. He believes I'm his father's man. He'll want someone loyal to him – someone who'll let him go to hell in a handcart his own way." He said the last in an undertone, but Jane heard him well enough.

"*If* he inherits."

Fitzwilliam winced. "Please, don't mention that. You never know who might overhear. Tonight, it is only the viscountess and the Honourable Miss Felix, but that all changes tomorrow with Lord Withers's arrival."

He was right. She couldn't act like she had over the first few days of her stay in what had been a practically empty house. "Sorry."

They entered the dining room. The table had been laid with particular splendour: towers of white roses and candles, white ribbons, and gleaming silverware. They took their assigned places at the table. Parks and his team moved in to serve as soon as all were in position.

Jane found she was not required to participate in conversation. Left alone as a person completely without importance, so obscure no one would ever remember her name once she was gone, Jane was able to enjoy her food. There were three courses, each containing at least ten dishes in a dizzying variety: soups and salmon, meats and macaroni, peas and potatoes, syllabubs and sauces, puddings and preserves. A little dish appeared near Sir Charles containing more spicy items, but otherwise it seemed Lady Cromwell had for once got her wish to have traditional fare for a fashionable dinner party. For the third course, the cloth was removed and the table reset with fruits and sweetmeats. In the centre towered a birthday cake for the heir, decorated with marzipan galloping horses. Jane barely had room but nobly managed to cram in a slice. It truly was the best meal she had ever eaten.

It was a shame, she was later to reflect, that it was the last dinner she would eat in peace at Southmoor.

Chapter 22

The ladies retired from the table to take tea in the parlour, leaving the gentlemen to their brandy, port, and cigars. Jane trailed behind the other females, wondering if she would be missed if she went to bed. Very full meant very sleepy, and no one needed her.

A soft touch on her arm surprised her out of her half-doze.

"Miss Austen?"

Annette had waited for her in the shadows of the staircase.

"Miss Felix?"

"Would you show me the library now?" Annette nodded to Lady Cromwell and her mother. "I don't think they will miss us, do you?" The two ladies were already seated on the sofa, and Lady Cromwell was displaying her latest silk project with more animation than she had shown all day. The viscountess was either genuinely interested or a very good actress. "And I hate to go to bed without something decent to read."

"Of course, my lady." Jane led the way, taking up a candlestick from the hall table.

Jane entered the darkened chamber and set about lighting the candles so Annette could admire it.

"This is as magnificent as I thought," declared Annette, holding her hands to her breast as she admired the cases of books, the globe that stood in a wooden stand like a giant's cup-and-ball game, the desks for letter-writing, the racks of the latest prints. "I could almost marry him for this," she added, though Jane suspected she wasn't supposed to have heard that remark.

"Is there any book in particular you wanted?" she asked instead.

"Oh no, part of the pleasure is just browsing." Annette ran her fingers along the first row of leather-bound books. "How strange."

"What is, my lady?"

"The way these are ordered – geography sits next to biography next to a novel."

Jane joined her and saw that she was right. "It is a very old library. Some of the works might even have come from the monastery. Perhaps they are shelved by the date they were added to the collection?"

"Then what is Fanny Burney doing here in this case?" Annette was standing by the second bookcase. "This is her most recent novel."

Her first theory had to be abandoned. Jane made a quick count of the cases in the room and noted the busts of the famous men that topped each one. The answer, when she saw it, was obvious. "It's alphabetical. Here under the bust of Aristotle are the authors beginning with A. Under the head of Boethius is Bacon."

"And Boccaccio and Burney and Burns – I do believe you are right." Annette wandered on, coming to a stop before the model steam engine in front of the next case. "And what's this?"

"That's a little engine made by one of the Abbey servants – a kind of toy. I believe it is going to be demonstrated on Saturday for the gentlemen."

Annette gave a sniff as if she didn't think very much of that. She opened the lid of the boiler and then the door of the furnace. "Hmm, I see. Very ingenious. Tell me, Miss Austen, what do you think of this place?" She spun the wheel.

"This place?" Jane asked warily. She hadn't quiet fathomed whose side Annette was on.

"The Abbey, stolen by jolly old King Henry and given to one of his favourites. Did you know he put out on the road the monks sworn to share their goods in common, and tend the sick, all to enrich one man? Does that not strike you as monstrous?" She flicked the wheel to go faster and faster.

"I think Henry guilty of crimes and cruelties too many to mention," agreed Jane – she had strong opinions about the monarchs of the land. "I believe he was a man of no religion and little can be said in his defence."

Annette paused in her spinning and turned to look properly at Jane, possibly for the first time. "Oh, bravo, Miss Austen. I wish you had the task of writing the history books. I admire plain speaking."

Jane decided that Annette was all right – like Fitzwilliam, Deepti, and Luke, rather than the Cromwells. "Are you going to marry Mr Cromwell?"

The lady smiled to herself. "That serves me right! I encourage plain speaking but hesitate when it comes to my turn. Yes, Miss Austen, I am considering the match. He comes from a good family – a line that goes back to Oliver Cromwell himself. My mother thinks it a fault but I would see it as an attraction."

"And do you wish to marry?" Jane asked.

"Now that is an interesting question." Lady Annette leaned so she was resting on the edge of the steam engine table. "You didn't ask if I wanted to marry Mr Cromwell, as one might expect, but whether I wanted to marry at all. No, I don't want to marry. I have no romantic feelings for any man and no desire to have children."

"So why are you considering it?" Jane would've thought a daughter of a viscountess would have a choice if anyone did.

She gave a little shrug, bony shoulders rising and falling. "Because it is what others want, but I dislike feeling like a sheep that is being herded into a pen by a pack of dogs and whistling shepherds. And Cromwell understands this. He knows me – knows that a match is the only way we can be truly free of all this." She waved her hand to the library.

"I thought you liked books?"

"I meant social obligations. I want to keep the books." Annette laughed at herself. "Yes, I know. I'm such a hypocrite."

Jane waited patiently while the lady chose a selection of volumes, ranging from a big tome the size of a family Bible to a slim collection of poetry.

"This should keep me happy," Annette said. "I'm going straight up to my room. If you return to the parlour, please give my excuses. I'm fatigued from my journey."

What a hummer of a lie! thought Jane admiringly. She was merely eager to start her bedtime reading. "I will, my lady. Sleep well."

Jane extinguished the candles and carried the candlestick she had brought with her back to the hall. Entering the parlour, she saw that Sir Charles, Lady Cromwell, and Lady Felix were playing cards, Fitzwilliam making up the fourth. There was no sign of the birthday boy.

"Miss Felix? Gone to bed?" said Lady Cromwell, as if going to bed before eleven was an unheard-of thing.

"She said the journey had tired her. Might I also retire?" asked Jane hopefully.

"You aren't required any more tonight. Oh, hearts were trumps? I quite forgot!" The lady's face fell as the cards were gathered up by Lady Felix.

"Do pay attention, dearest," snapped Sir Charles. Lady Felix and Fitzwilliam were beating them hands down. "Stop distracting her, girl."

Considering herself dismissed, Jane escaped for what was to be the last quiet moment at Southmoor.

Chapter 28

A whistle was sounding. Rousing from sleep in the pitch-black night, Jane couldn't at first make out what she was hearing – sharp, brassy, familiar…

The steam engine!

Leaping out of bed, Jane dashed into the corridor. She wasn't the first: Deepti and her father stood there, both cloaked with lantern in hand.

"The library!" said Jane.

Understanding, they followed her as she ran down the stairs. Smoke was seeping out from under the door. Jane was about to throw it open when Arjun caught her by the back of her nightdress.

"Careful!" he said. He put his palm against the door, checking for heat. Satisfied, he opened it. Jane coughed as yet more smoke billowed. Flickers of flame appeared where they really should not be, over by the wall where the bookcases were. The model engine must have caught fire; the flames had spread to the tablecloth and nearest shelves.

"Stay back!" warned Arjun, pushing his daughter and Jane away. "Sound the alarm!" He ripped the nearest curtain down from its rails and threw it over the shuddering, shrieking model.

Jane ran back to the floor above. "Fire!" she shouted, but her voice sounded thin on first attempt. She cleared her throat. "Fire!" she tried again, banging on doors. Down below, Deepti struck the dinner gong repeatedly.

The Cromwells and their guests stumbled out into the corridor from their various rooms. The ladies were in their nightclothes, though Sir Charles was still dressed.

He seized Jane's shoulders. "What's the meaning of this?"

"Fire – in the library!"

He let go and took off.

"Oh, oh," said Lady Cromwell, flapping about in her lacy nightdress like a headless chicken. "A fire! Here! Oh my!"

Jane realized someone needed to take control and it looked like that was going to have to be her. "Lady Felix, the library is at the west end of the building. The parlour is the safest refuge I can think of."

Lady Felix gave her a nod. "Very good. Annette, fetch your wrap. We'll go to the parlour until we have the all-clear."

Jane went into Lady Cromwell's room, which was amazingly untidy – piles of magazines, books, and clothes on every surface. Anyone would think the lady did not have a household of staff picking up after her. She grabbed a warm shawl, which she then wrapped around the lady's shoulders. "Ma'am, if you would go down, I'll see what news I can bring you."

Like a docile child, Lady Cromwell obeyed, following her guests to the parlour.

Jane spent a moment to return to her own room and put on her boots and a dressing gown. She then attempted to return to the library via the back stairs, only to find her way blocked by a chain of servants hauling buckets. She retraced her steps and approached from the entrance hall. Cromwell and Fitzwilliam were dragging out the remains of a rug. They cast it on to the gravel and stamped out the last smouldering fibres.

"Is there much damage?" asked Jane.

"We lost a table and most of one bookcase," said Cromwell. "It hasn't spread, thank heavens. Credit goes to Arjun and his daughter for raising the alarm so swiftly." He wiped a sleeve across his face.

Jane opened her mouth to mention that she had been the first but closed it. If Sir Charles felt he owed Arjun and Deepti, maybe he would send for their family? She went instead to give her report to the guests.

Viscountess Felix received it like a general a report from a battlefield. "Thank you, Miss... er..."

"Jane Austen," said Jane.

"Miss Austen. Old places like these are fire hazards. I lost a wing of my castle in Scotland thanks to a careless housekeeper last year." She said this to Lady Cromwell as a kind of commiseration. "It can happen to anyone."

If they had a castle, thought Jane.

Parks came in, gave his own reassuring report, and took orders for warm drinks. Cromwell and Fitzwilliam entered, streaked with soot, and were greeted as heroes. The parlour began to have quite a festive air as it was realized that no major harm had been done. Annette was lamenting the loss of the books in the Caesar bookshelf, but everyone else was happy to escape with their lives. Cromwell even went so far as to tease her that she would prefer to lose him than the works of Cicero, and she pretended to think seriously about it for a moment.

"You may be right," she said, causing much laughter.

The fun lasted until Sir Charles came into the room, bringing his own storm cloud.

"My apologies, my lady, Miss Felix," he said sternly, "for the inconvenience."

"All's well, Sir Charles?" said Viscountess Felix.

"Not entirely." Sir Charles moved stiffly to stand in the centre of the room. "The fire did not start on its own. Someone saw fit to go into the library in the dead of night, set a model steam engine running, and leave it until it overheated. The blasted thing runs on oil so of course it set the place alight. We could have all been burned to a frazzle if my servants hadn't heard the alarm." He tossed back a glass of brandy. "So it therefore remains to find and punish the evildoer. And don't you fear, I will find out who did this and I will punish that individual to the fullness of the powers invested me as local magistrate."

Jane gulped. She knew she was innocent but she also realized she was the last one to have been in the library that evening, aside from the person who started the machine, of course. How long would it take for Sir Charles to find that out? And when he did, would he blame her?

Just when she thought that the nightmare could not get any worse, Scroop, the head groom, burst into the room.

"Sir, sir!"

"What is it, man?" demanded Sir Charles.

"Romeo – Arachne – they're both missing from the stables! They've been stolen!"

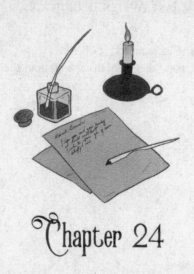

Chapter 24

Pandemonium followed on this announcement. Sir Charles sent every able-bodied man, woman, and child that he could command out into the grounds with all the lanterns in the house, instructed to look for any trace of the horse thieves. Only his guests and his wife were exempt – and only because he couldn't issue orders to them. Jane wondered if she had escaped Sir Charles's notice, but no. As a final thought, Sir Charles dispatched her to get her "infernal hound" and see if he could sniff out any trace of the precious creatures. Sir Charles must really be scraping the barrel if he thought she and Grandison could make a difference, Jane decided.

In contrast to the house in chaos, a deathly silence reigned in the stables, bar the fretting of the remaining horses as they sensed all was not well in their home. Jane took Grandison to sniff Arachne's loose box but with little hope he'd be able to do anything with it. He'd not been trained to follow a trail – in fact, he hadn't really been trained to do very much at all. Cromwell had already left with the hounds and the pack-master so they were far more likely to pick up a trace. Grandison was happy to pretend he could track like a bloodhound, though, because this brought him the unexpected bonus of a night-time walk.

"Arachne," Jane said encouragingly. "Nice horse. Sugar lumps."

Grandison sniffed the ground for a moment and then bounded away toward the nearest lantern to greet another searcher. This turned out to be Parks, who yelped as the dog leaped up to say hello. Parks clearly wasn't at ease outside his little butler kingdom of the house and was restricting his search to the area closest to it. He appeared to be studying the gravel for hoof prints.

"Grandison, down! Any news?" asked Jane.

"No, Miss, but I just saw Sir Charles take his musket to go and question the travellers. He thinks they'll have connections to shady folk – the kind that would know what to do with stolen property."

Jane grimaced. "He's not likely to get a friendly reception if he charges in there in the middle of the night blaming them."

"I fear you are right, Miss, but he sees plots everywhere and strangers are the first he suspects. He thinks that whoever took the horses set the fire as a diversion and then stole them away while we were all putting out the flames."

That made sense, apart from one important fact. "But how would the travellers know about the steam engine?"

"Indeed, Miss. I think Sir Charles is so angry right now, he can't reason this through with a cool head."

Grandison barked and ran off into the dark.

Jane sighed. "I'd better go after him."

Parks gave a sad shake of his head. "You shouldn't be out here alone. If there are thieves about and you spot them, whatever you do, don't approach them! These are desperate people!"

Grandison led Jane into the Abbey ruins, where he proceeded to bounce around on the trapdoor from where he had rescued her earlier, woofing merrily.

"Yes, yes, clever dog."

Had that only been last night? It felt like days had passed.

He loped off into the darkness, probably on another rabbit chase. This was hopeless. The ruins were deserted and she was achieving nothing here – not to mention that the candle in her lantern was nearly burned out. Jane whistled, Grandison gambolled back, and they headed for the stables. It made more sense to search in daylight, thought Jane. All Sir Charles was achieving at the moment was ensuring his people stamped out any footprints or muddled other clues in their eagerness to help.

A stone's throw from the stable, Grandison's happy trot froze. He sniffed, nose in the air, growled, and then bolted straight toward the stable door.

Had the horses been found? Jane picked up her skirts and ran after him.

But it wasn't horses that had brought Grandison racing back: it was a *horse*whip!

Chapter 25

Scroop had Luke by the ear, threatening him with a beating.

That man was a FIEND!

"How dare you leave the horses!" Scroop bellowed. "You were supposed to guard them with your life!"

As Scroop brought the whip down, Grandison leaped and took it clean from his hand.

Oh, well done, Grandison!

The groom swore horribly, threatening the dog with all manner of grisly ends if he didn't return the whip, but Grandison danced away, treating the whip like a stick he had rightfully won.

"But it weren't my fault, Mr Scroop!" protested Luke. "You said everyone had to go help with the fire!"

"You should've known that it didn't mean you! Your job is here – you're to guard the horses at night!" Deprived of his whip, Scroop shook Luke.

Grandison ran back to Jane and dropped the whip at her feet. She picked it up and tucked it out of sight in a fold of her skirt.

"Let go of him, Mr Scroop," she said firmly.

"Or what, Miss?" sneered the groom.

Jane racked her brains for a threat he would respect. "Or I'll tell Mr Fitzwilliam, who will report your behaviour to his father."

Scroop released his hold on Luke, disgust curling his lips. "It won't matter. If something has happened to those horses, none of us will have a job next week."

"Hadn't you better go look for them then?" said Jane, thinking it best that the groom and Luke were separated for the rest of the night.

"I was sent back with the boy. We're supposed to be guarding what's left of the horses, in case the thieves return." Scroop shot a vicious look at Luke. "You can't hide behind her skirts for ever, boy. You've got a reckoning coming." With that threat, he stamped away.

Luke turned from Jane and kicked a bucket across the yard. "They're going to blame me. It's not fair!"

Jane knew this was a crisis beyond the comfort of barley sugars. "Why you?"

He punched the wall, which must have hurt him far more than the bricks. "Because I'm a fatherless stray they took in; that's what they call me – a stray! I'm sick of it! They say I'm the result of sin – always in the wrong." Luke leaned against the wall, his shoulders heaving. "It's not bloody fair! I love those horses. I wouldn't hurt them – would stop anyone if I could. Arachne doesn't like the dark. Romeo, he needs special handling. They'll be terrified with strangers."

"I'm sorry, Luke."

"It's too late for sorry. I'll be lucky if they just turn me out. It was my machine that caught fire – it won't take Sir Charles long to remember that." He stood up and looked about him desperately. "I've got to go – run now before they come for me."

That sounded like a very bad idea to Jane. "Won't they just use that as proof you were involved?"

"So I just sit here and let them blame me?"

Put like that, his choices were terrible. "Is there no one who'll speak up for you? Parks?"

"Mr Parks rules in the house. Mr Scroop rules out here."

"Mr Fitzwilliam the steward then? I've heard he's a fair man," offered Jane.

"You don't know what it's like, Miss. It doesn't matter what Mr Parks, or Mr Fitzwilliam, or even King George himself thinks; it's what Sir Charles thinks – and he already reckons I'm a trouble-maker. And now I've failed him."

"You weren't to know thieves would take advantage of the fire."

"But I should've done. I should've been a bleeding mind reader, according to Mr Scroop." He kicked the bucket again, this time breaking off the handle as it tumble-turned.

She had to divert his attention away from anger so he could see clear to help himself.

"All right. I agree. Then we must find the horses ourselves. Sir Charles is going about this all wrong."

That got Luke's attention. "What?"

"He's sent everyone out without a plan. If there were any clues left, they'll be walked over ten times before dawn. He should have started with the 'who?', not the 'where?'. If he knew who the thief was, then he would know where to look. At the moment he is going about, casting accusations left, right, and centre. He's putting off witnesses from coming forward – a completely blockheaded way of beginning his search."

Her disrespectful tone helped calm Luke a little. "Did you just say that Sir Charles is a blockhead?"

"Yes, and a bully. You stay out of his way – and Scroop's – and meet me as soon as it is fully light in the ruins. Once Sir Charles calls off the search, we'll take over."

Luke gave her an odd look. "You and me?"

"Why not?"

"What do we know about finding horses?"

"We'll do better than Sir Charles's search party. You know the horses and I'm good at finding things out, according to my family."

"That means they think you're nosey."

She didn't dignify that with a reply. "There's no reason why I can't turn my skill to larger things, like who stole the horses. Now, have you got somewhere safe to hide – a place where they won't think you're running away?"

"I'll go up to the hayloft. If they say I've run for it, I can explain that I was hiding to catch the thieves in action if they returned."

Jane nodded. That was a good, plausible excuse. "I'm going back to the house to get a few hours' sleep and then return properly dressed. If we are going horse-hunting, I'd prefer not to be in my dressing gown. Grandison, stay! Guard!" She pointed to Luke.

Her dog whined once, circled, and sat down across the entrance to the empty stable that had once held the two prize horses.

Better late than never, thought Jane, heading back to the house, though maybe it was more a case of shutting the stable door after the horse had bolted.

Chapter 26

Surprisingly, Jane managed a couple of hours' sleep. Having spent the previous night in a hole, and this one fighting fires and searching for horses, her body had reached its limit and shut down as soon as her head hit the pillow. When she woke, it was early morning, the house resting in an exhausted silence. No water for washing had been brought up so she made do with the cold leftovers in her jug, splashing her face to drive away fatigue.

As her mind woke, questions started forming. There were the obvious ones of "Who set the machine running?" and "Who stole the horses?", but also "Who had been walking abroad the two previous nights with a lantern?". Her old assumption was that it had been someone playing on the fear of the Abbey ghost, for fun or for malice, but now a new motive had arisen: had the person been preparing the way for the theft? The London papers often carried spine-chilling tales of housebreakers spying on their targets before a burglary; had the lantern-carrier been checking the stables and the entry points to the house? It could have nothing to do with the legend of the ghost at all.

Jane took her notebook and newly sharpened pencil to go down to the library. The sequence of events had started there so that was where she would begin before going out to find Luke. The library looked a sorry place this morning: plaster ceiling stained with black, the mouldings of fruits, flowers, and leaves now like the blighted goods a market stallholder had not been able to sell. The table that held the steam engine had been dragged out, as had the carpet that lay nearest to it. Of the engine there was no sign, but Jane guessed that had been disposed of in a similar rough fashion.

She made a note to find out where it was so Luke could examine it.

One odd detail was the candlestick she remembered replacing on the hall table. It was on a side table. Had one of the servants brought it with them when they fought the fire? That seemed a little unlikely. It was more plausible that the fire-starter had carried it in. Jane made a note.

The Caesar bookshelf was burned beyond salvaging. Books had been pulled from the shelf and doused with water – priceless volumes, some of them handwritten medieval texts. No book lover could have purposely caused this carnage. The acrid smell of wet ash filled the air. As far as she could see, the room only told her what she already knew: the machine had set the nearest bookcase on fire. Not directly, of course, but likely first the cloth on the table had gone up, then the carpet, and in turn the lowest shelf.

The beauty of the machine was that the fire-setter could start it, walk away, and be busy about the theft far from the scene of his first crime.

But her question from the night before came back to her. Who had known that the model was even here? Sir Charles had charged off to blame the fair people as likely horse-thieves, but what knowledge did they have about the contents of his library? The only people who knew the model was here were the family and the staff. Annette too, of course, as Jane had brought her here but a few hours ago. There was a further step in the mystery: who would have the knowledge to work the engine? Luke, Fitzwilliam definitely, and the people who had watched the demonstration, herself included; and again, possibly Annette, as she had looked at it as if she could puzzle out how it worked.

Jane paused, pencil hovering over her notebook. What about the fire being a coincidence? Had Annette come back to satisfy her curiosity and been too scared to admit that she had been tampering?

Jane shook her head and crossed that out. The lady didn't seem the kind to run away from trouble. She would've dealt with it, or at least raised the alarm.

A noise from the end of the room startled her. Fitzwilliam rose from a winged chair that had hidden him from her gaze. A blanket dropped to the floor.

"What are you doing here?" Jane asked.

"I could ask you the same thing." He yawned and ran his fingers through his already dishevelled hair.

"I asked first."

He rolled his head as if his neck pained him. "If you want the truth, I'm hiding. Sir Charles wouldn't let me go to bed without first giving him news of his horses. I came in here to catch forty winks. I'm useless to anyone if I'm so tired I can't see straight."

"So you chose a room that reeks of smoke?"

"Yes, because no one in their right minds would come in here to sleep. What about you?"

Jane tucked her notebook away. "I'm investigating."

"What are you investigating?"

"The fire, of course!"

"Why?"

"Because if we find out who set it, then we'll have a clue as to who stole the horses."

"You think that the same person did this?" He gestured to the burned bookcase.

"It isn't likely that two such things could happen on the same night and not be connected," Jane reasoned.

"Isn't it? Have you looked at what was lost?"

"I can see it with my own eyes. Lots of lovely books by authors beginning with 'C'."

"You are missing the point." Fitzwilliam shook his head.

"Then perhaps you'll tell me then, as I'm too slow to work it out?"

"Cromwell begins with 'C' – the family papers were shelved under 'Caesar'."

"You mean the land deeds – the wills – all the material you used in your history?" This was becoming more exciting by the minute.

"That's right. Every document this family has kept since the time of Henry VIII – Sir Charles is yet to realize the seriousness of what was lost and I am not volunteering to remind him." He folded his arms. "So,

Miss Austen, do you still think this is about the little matter of the horse theft?"

Chapter 27

Leaving Fitzwilliam still hiding out in the soggy library, Jane hurried down the servants' staircase. The favourite of her ideas had held neatly together until she had talked to Fitzwilliam: she had come around to the idea that the thief had spent the last few nights masquerading as the Abbey ghost, had set the steam engine going as a diversion, and stolen the horses while the servants were too busy – or too scared if they saw his monk's habit – to look at him too closely. Now she was in a quandary. Which was the main crime: stealing Romeo and Arachne or getting rid of the evidence concerning the inheritance? Were the two linked or pure coincidence?

She didn't have enough clues either way – and Luke was waiting for her in the ruins. Perhaps she should stop in the kitchen and grab some rolls for breakfast?

As she passed the door that gave on to the entrance hall, raised voices caught her attention.

Eavesdroppers never heard anything to their own good, her mother always said. Jane had her own saying, though: *eavesdroppers always heard lots of interesting things so shouldn't worry about that*.

"You cannot seriously expect the party to go ahead as if nothing has happened!" That was Sir Charles. Jane caught a glimpse of him through the crack in the door. He was mud-splattered and soot-stained, hair wild. He hadn't been to bed or paused to change since the fire in the library.

"But, dearest, it is Wicky's special day," coaxed Lady Cromwell. Jane could see a little slice of her, just a white hand reaching out to pat her husband's arm. "What good, my love, can cancelling the party and the ball do? You've sent out men to search for the horses on all the local roads. The thieves won't get far. While we wait for news, we should carry on as usual."

"But I don't feel like celebrating!"

"Sir, I'm sorry about the horses – you know I am." So Cromwell was there too. Jane couldn't see him though, just hear his persuasive tones as he acted his most charming self. "By the Lord Harry, one of them was about to be mine, wasn't she?"

Sir Charles grunted, not exactly agreeing but at least noting his son's point.

"So, by rights this is half my loss too and I'm rising above it. We can't do any more than we've done, and I'll only come of age once –"

"Thank heaven," growled Sir Charles. "I'll be shot of the responsibility for you tomorrow. No more bills landing on my desk."

Cromwell carried on as if he hadn't heard his father's slight. "The arrangements for the festivities are made. I suppose we could annoy our tenants and cancel the party today – they aren't people who matter in the grand scheme of things – but you'd be telling them you value their enjoyment less than two horses."

"But that's true!"

"It might be true, but do you want them to know that? You're the one always going on to me about the landowner's responsibilities to his people."

"Humph."

Cromwell had scored a hit, noted Jane.

"And as for the ball, things are too far gone to cancel. The Felixes are here, Lord Withers will already be on the road, as are many of the other guests. Do you want to snub so many people of influence by turning them away as soon as they arrive?"

"Darling, we must show them a brave face and carry on regardless," added Lady Cromwell. "Come now, get some rest. Hopefully there will be better news by the time you wake."

"All right, all right," growled Sir Charles. "I suppose you two won't give me any peace if I don't let this farce carry on. Have the party – but don't expect me to enjoy a single moment of it!"

"Father, that has never been my expectation," said Cromwell wryly.

A door slammed.

"Your father will enjoy it once he resigns himself to the fact he can't do any more," said Lady Cromwell.

"To be honest, Mama, I don't care tuppence if he enjoys himself. I always knew he loved those blasted horses more than me so I can't say he doesn't deserve this. I intend to enjoy my party."

The two parted, leaving the entrance hall clear. Jane crept out and checked that the candlestick had indeed been moved from where she had left it. That suggested the fire-starter had come this way. Jane hurried on, snagged two rolls from the kitchen, and left by the back door.

Luke and Grandison were waiting for her in the tumbled-down nave. Jane threw the boy a roll, which he caught with impressive reflexes. She chucked the dog a crust broken off hers.

"Breakfast," she said, biting into her roll.

"Thank you, Miss."

Grandison barked, hoping for more.

"That's it for the moment. Go and play." Jane shooed him away. The dog trotted off. "Any news this morning?"

"No, Miss. The search parties came back at first light, but Sir Charles has left guards on all the roads and main footpaths. The horses won't be taken out of the area without anyone noticing."

"Then they're probably still close by," said Jane, half to herself.

"Have you any ideas who did it – the fire and the theft?" Luke brushed off a fallen stone for her to sit on.

"I ran into Fitzwilliam this morning before I came out here. He thinks it's possible the two aren't linked – just a strange coincidence. Do you know what time the horses went missing?"

Luke flicked the crumbs from his lap. "No, I don't. All of us were working late, preparing for the arrivals expected tomorrow. I didn't get to my bed, or otherwise I'd've seen if Romeo was in his stable."

So Mr Scroop was the one who had taken Luke off night guard duty – and then had the gall to blame him!

"Then we heard the gong up at the house and we all rushed over."

"Do you remember who you saw?"

"Just the other lads…"

"Anyone missing?"

Luke scrunched up his nose, thinking. "Not that I remember."

"And at the house?"

"Mr Cromwell was just entering the front door from the garden. I thought he might have been with the fair people, as he had a garland of flowers in his hair and looked tipsy. Mr Fitzwilliam came in from the kitchen. Then there were the house servants – Mr Parks, the footmen, some of the maids. Oh, and the Indian girl was in the hall banging on the gong until Sir Charles told her to stop the racket."

Jane tried to remember whom she had seen. On the bedroom floor, it had been the guests, Sir Charles, and Lady Cromwell. On the stairs, she'd run into the servants, but how many of them were present was hard to know in the smoke and noise. Any one of them could've slipped away and claimed to have been there all the time.

But Deepti and Arjun had already been awake and dressed when she got up. They'd been holding lanterns. *Why have a light unless you were planning to go out – or had just come back…?*

Chapter 28

Jane didn't like the direction in which her thoughts were running. She already knew Arjun and Deepti wished to reunite their family and that was expensive, costing more than they could earn in several years of serving the family. Had they decided to take this shortcut, sell the horses, and return to India where no one could follow?

"What's wrong, Miss? You look like you've sat on a pin."

"There's someone I need to ask something. Have you seen Deepti?"

"No, but I know where she'll be shortly. The servants are going to the tenants' party at midday for a few hours, before they have to carry on with preparations for the ball."

"Good. Let's have a look for tracks before everyone else is up and about."

But it was as Jane suspected; any trail had been ruined by the passage of scores of feet last night. There were hoof prints on the lawn, which Luke swore were Romeo's, but they could've been left from his ride with Sir Charles the day before. Luke thought he spotted the smaller imprint of Arachne near the ruins but the trace was too vague for him to be sure.

On the lawn that was to be the ballroom tomorrow, Jane stood, hands on hips, and surveyed the scene. The ruins were behind her, a wood to her right, in front the field where the party was soon going to take place, and the stables to her left. If the horses had been led this way, where would she have taken them? Into the trees? The wood must've been searched, but it had been night-time so it was definitely worth another look.

"Do you know any places where someone could stable two horses in the woods?"

Luke dug his hands in his pockets. "I suppose there's the old gamekeeper's cottage. That's bound to have been checked."

"Let's have a look anyway."

"It's a rough path, Miss, and I didn't think fine ladies liked tramping through woods. You might tear your dress."

Jane gave Luke an exasperated look. "Luke, this is a serious investigation and a couple of tears in a petticoat are the least of our worries. Lives are at stake." She glanced down at her serviceable cotton skirt. "Besides, this is my third-best gown, recently my fourth, and it's used to such treatment."

Luke frowned, working that out. "What happened to the last third-best?"

"It became my second."

"And the second?"

"I could tell you but then I'd have to kill you."

"You're daft, Miss."

"No, I'm just an Austen – which means I'm much more outrageous than you can possibly imagine."

They were walking toward the woods now, Grandison gambolling beside them.

"Outrageous?" Luke sounded intrigued.

"When you meet my sister and brothers, you'll understand. I'm just the least strange and most sensible of the lot."

He gave her another look. "Now that I don't believe."

She'd better change the subject. "Look about you, Luke. Can you see any tracks?"

He rolled his eyes. "You're a bit bossy, do you know that?"

"I prefer 'decisive'."

"No, bossy is what you are." Grumbling, Luke did search as requested. The ground was damp so there were marks – horses, boots, fox and dog prints, but nothing distinct.

Jane heard a rip behind her and discreetly unhooked her skirt from a bramble, not wanting an "I told you so" from Luke. "Anything?"

"Could be. Let's press on to the gamekeeper's cottage." He forged ahead and pushed on though the low branches, forgetting to hold them for her. Grandison streaked after him.

Now who's being bossy? thought Jane, ducking a backswing from a holly twig. *When a girl says what to do, she's called bossy. If it is a boy, he's showing great leadership qualities.*

Thanks to Luke's knowledge of the woodland, they reached the cottage by the most direct route. It would've been hard, but not impossible, to bring two horses the same way, thought Jane, examining a broken twig next to the path. The cottage, however, was a slump of wooden frame and rotting thatch, no place for pedigree horses.

Luke climbed in through an empty window frame while Jane and Grandison walked around the building. Even to her untrained eye, she could see that people had been there recently. In front of what had been the old door were the black ashes of a campfire and some half-burned twigs. Grandison sniffed it enthusiastically before sneezing. She kneeled down. Not quite cold and not damp. She guessed that it had been lit last night by the search party.

"Miss, Miss, in here!"

Jane squeezed through the door, which hung off its hinges. Luke was kneeling by a pile of horse manure, poking it with a stick.

"I take it that is familiar?"

Luke grinned up at her. "I told you that being a stableboy meant being smeared with worse stuff than dog drool. Even I can't tell one horse dropping from another, but two different horses have definitely been in here recently – one in this spot, one tethered over there." He pointed to a smaller pile of dung. "I'm guessing that belongs to Arachne, and this Romeo."

At last: a clue! Jane wanted to dance on the spot. "But they must've been gone before the searchers reached here."

"Searchers?" asked Luke.

"There's a campfire by the front door."

"Or maybe that was left by the horse thieves?"

"Bold thieves to light a fire saying 'come and find us'. Why do you say 'thieves' rather than 'thief'?" asked Jane.

"Two horses – and Romeo acts up with strangers. It stands to reason it would take two people to lead them through the woods. You have to go single file."

Again, Jane had a picture of Deepti and her father standing cloaked and booted outside their room. They could've done it: the timing was right. They would've known the grounds well enough to find this place to hide the horses. They could've come back when the search was launched – might even have volunteered to search in this direction – and take the horses further off before the watch on the roads was set. But where to? They were back at the house now so they wouldn't have gone far.

If they had anything to do with it. Jane didn't like thinking them guilty of a hanging offence without more evidence. She had to take this step by step. Just because something was possible did not mean it was probable.

"If you were going to steal two valuable horses, Luke…" Jane began.

He stood and held up his hands. "I had nothing to do with it."

"I never said you did. In fact, I'm thinking you are the one person besides myself whom I know for sure to be innocent."

"How do you know that?"

"Because I know you care for the horses and wouldn't want them to suffer. Wherever they are now, it won't be as snug as their stable."

His cheeks flushed. "Thank you, Miss, for believing me."

"Please, call me Jane. We're partners now, after all."

"Partners?"

"In detection. Like the Bow Street Runners – though by all accounts they aren't very good at that part of their job enforcing the law in London. I would offer my hand to shake on it but…"

"I've just been poking dung?"

She nodded. "Shall we get back to the party? I have a few people I want to talk to."

Luke squeezed past the door. "Do you need me to open it further for you?"

"I got in so I'll get out." She paused. "Actually, have a go moving it. Let's see how strong someone had to be to get the horses in here."

"There's a knack to it." Luke grabbed the old handle. "You… have… to… lift… it." He let it drop down a foot wider and Jane walked through.

"So not impossible for a man or even a strong boy or girl to do?" She thought of weapon exercises.

"A boy, yes, but not a girl." Luke seemed confident about that but he was doubtless still thinking of fine ladies, not girls who worked as laundresses.

After pushing their way back through the wood, they arrived at the side of the field where the party was already underway. More time had passed than Jane expected.

"How long does it take to get to the cottage, Luke?"

He shrugged. "Ten minutes."

"With horses?"

"Maybe a little longer. Fifteen."

They had to find out who was missing for over thirty minutes last night – and that would be hard to do with so many coming and going into the house with buckets and taking out smouldering items.

A great cheer went up from the wrestling ring. A tall farmhand had just been defeated by the slight figure of the Indian cook. Almost at the same moment, a coach appeared at the top of the last bend in the drive before the house.

"More guests," said Luke. "They're early. I should see to the horses."

"Are you coming to the party?" asked Jane.

"I'd better stay out of sight. You know where to find me. Do you want me to take Grandison?"

Jane considered the pig roast and the beer tent – and the potential havoc a hungry dog could cause. "Please."

"Heel, boy." Luke jogged toward the stables, Grandison running obediently at his side.

Why would her dog not do that for her? Jane wondered, not for the first time.

Chapter 29

J ane knew where Arjun was but she had more difficulty spotting his daughter. Deepti wasn't watching the wrestling, marvelling at the rope walkers, or sampling the food by the cooking tent. Jane finally found her at the archery butts. She was dressed in a turquoise tunic and matching loose trousers, hair secured in a plait down her back. There were only two other girls taking part in the contest, both dressed in their Sunday best and giggling with their young men. Their arrows went far wide of the butts, even though they were allowed to go half the distance nearer than the competition line.

"Miss, do you want to fire from where the other young ladies stood?" asked the judge as Deepti came forward for her turn.

"No, thank you," she said.

"But it's a long way for a little miss like you."

"I want to enter the competition with the men."

"That's most irregular." He looked around him, gauging the reaction of the other competitors.

"It's not against the rules, is it?"

He appeared on the point of refusing when Cromwell bounded up, face bright with excitement.

"Hello, one and all. What's this? Deepti, isn't it? Want to enter along with the big boys, do you?" he said with hearty good cheer. "Let her try her hand, Rawlings, for the prize. No harm done, hey?"

Deepti nodded her thanks, picked three arrows from the quiver, and took aim. Jane could instantly see the difference between her and the previous contenders. The boys had handled the bow a little awkwardly. Deepti treated the bow like it was an extension of her body. She became one lethal weapon, releasing the arrow with no fuss or flourish, just a silent confidence. Approaching from the side, Jane was at the wrong angle to see where it struck, but she was unsurprised to hear applause ring out.

"Wonderful shot, Miss," said the judge, enthusiasm overcoming his earlier prejudice. "Can you do that again? You have three goes. The most accurate archer over all three at the end of the day wins the prize."

"I can try," said Deepti modestly.

Jane sped up so she could watch the final two shots. It was beautiful to witness: the fluid lining up of the arrow, the brief flight, and the solid thump as they sprouted beside the first.

"I don't think anyone could beat that, do you, Rawlings?" said Cromwell. His gaze fell on Jane. "And you, Miss Austen, are you a fair hand at the bow too? Are all the ladies at Southmoor Artemises and Amazons?"

Jane hadn't tried since she'd used a toy one made for her brother Francis; that had done more damage to the washing than targets. "I always like to think I'd be good at something before I try but experience usually proves me wrong."

"I can show you how," said Deepti.

"You can use the butt at the end," said the judge, turning his attention back to his other customers.

Deepti selected three more arrows and walked Jane over to the target. "The most important thing is to remember how to stand." She passed Jane her forearm guard. "You'll need this or the string will hurt your arm."

Jane slipped it on. "I see your father is doing as well at wrestling as you are at archery."

"It is what we are trained to do," said Deepti. "It is not really fair, going up against farmers and field workers when we are warriors."

"But you do so anyway?"

Deepti flashed her a quick grin. "Yes – there's money to be won and we need it."

Jane noted that there was no hint that Deepti or her father expected to come into riches soon, which would have been the case if they had the horses hidden somewhere.

"You want to leave England?" She twanged the string as if the question were a casual one.

"My father hopes to bring my mother and brothers here because he earns better wages than he would in India, but I want to go home," Deepti said, adjusting Jane's stance. "We argue about that a lot. Now, remember, that the arrow does not fly straight." She sketched an arch in the air. "Bring the string back to your cheek as close to your ear as you can. Don't wobble! Better. And – let go."

Jane let the string ping from her fingers. She feared she had wobbled at the last moment.

"Not bad," said Deepti, "for a first attempt."

Her arrow had just hit the bottom of the target. The Austen honour was safe.

"Raise the tip a little and try again."

Jane obeyed.

"By the cheek, remember. You should be looking down the arrow as if you are about to fly with it."

Jane released the string and the arrow hit the second ring.

"Better!" Deepti applauded.

"It's not so difficult, is it?" said Jane. Just to prove her wrong, the final arrow sailed over the top of the target and hit the straw bales stacked behind to catch such misfires. "Oh."

Deepti smiled. "You got too confident, Jane." Jane liked hearing her first name from her new friend. It was almost like having a sister here. "You have to practise day after day, in all weathers, before you can master it."

"I'm not sure Mama would approve of that." Jane entertained a brief fantasy of turning the rectory lawn into an archery field. Her brothers would approve of the new entertainment but not her parents, who liked to take the sun without fear of being struck by errant arrows. "Thank you for showing me. Shall we go and see how your father is getting on?"

Deepti put the bow back on the rack. "Oh, he'll win."

"You're so certain?"

"Yes." It wasn't arrogance but confidence speaking. "Sir Charles hired him because he was the best at what he did."

"What was Sir Charles doing in India?" asked Jane.

"He came to buy Romeo."

Chapter 30

Of course, it would be about horses! That was the only thing that Sir Charles really cared about. "And he went all the way to India to get him?"

Deepti set off up the slope toward the wrestling. "Romeo is no ordinary stallion. There is a legendary breed of racehorses from Arabia, belonging to the family of the great Mughal emperor Jahangir. These horses were never given to outsiders."

"But Sir Charles got one?"

"Yes." Deepti wrinkled her nose in disdain. "The great families, even Jahangir's dynasty, are now only a shadow of what they once were. They struggle to hold on to little kingdoms. One of these got in debt to the Company. Sir Charles saw his chance. He negotiated a favourable settlement for the maharajah because he knew the right people in the Company. Romeo was his price. Many people were against it and there was fear that these enemies would kill the horse rather than see it go to England, so my father was hired."

"He was engaged to protect Romeo?"

Deepti nodded. "And Sir Charles. Assassins made two attempts to kill man and horse before they could leave the country. He owes my father his life but he does not remember his debts."

Deepti was describing an exotic world about which Jane knew only from travellers' tales. Assassins creeping up on jungle encampments in the dead of night, the roar of the tiger, the neigh of terrified horses… Jane shivered. "I wouldn't forget such a debt."

"No, *you* wouldn't." Deepti smiled.

Jane should have realized that a household that could call a Persian cat the most English name of "Muffin" was likely to disguise an Arabian thoroughbred as an Italian star-crossed lover.

"You didn't steal the horses, did you?" Jane had blurted out the question before she had quite realized that she was speaking her thoughts aloud.

"You suspected us?" Deepti stiffened, friendliness vanishing.

Jane felt ashamed. "I'm sorry, but I wondered why you and your father were dressed and holding lanterns when I met you outside our rooms. I didn't want it to be you – and I don't think it was, not now I've talked to you. You both have too much honour."

Deepti gave a curt nod. "Thank you for saying that. I am not offended. Suspicion is not always wrong – a bodyguard must be wary of everyone. A friendly approach might be the cloak for an assassin."

"We don't get many of those in Hampshire."

"Do you not? I always thought that bad people are to be found everywhere. But I will tell you why we were awake. We were going out for a night-time walk. My father is teaching me the stars and how to find my way in the dark."

"But you'd not gone out yet so you didn't see anything?"

"Sadly not. My father is very upset that he missed the chance of catching the thief."

"If your father had still been in charge of Romeo's safety, I doubt anyone would've got past him."

"No, they would not."

A man flew by Jane, having been ejected from the wrestling ring by Arjun.

"Oh, well done, the cook!" called Cromwell, who appeared to be getting everywhere at his own party. Annette was on his arm, watching the sport with serious interest as if she, like Jane, would later take notes. "Anyone else wish to take on our champion? No? Then the prize –"

"Not so fast, Cromwell!" Two young gentlemen were hastening from the house to the wrestling ring. As they were the size of haystacks, Jane guessed these were the sons of Lord Withers. "We want a go!" said one.

"Jamieson, Raleigh, this is only a little country match – not up to your level," said Cromwell with a challenging glint in his eye. "I'm sure you'll find much more skilled opponents in London."

The Withers brothers exchanged a look and began stripping down to their shirts and breeches.

"One at a time!" laughed Cromwell.

"Of course! We're no cheats. Got to give the blighter a chance," said one. "Miss Felix." He bowed to Cromwell's companion.

"Lord Jamieson," said the lady, dipping a curtsey. "Mr Raleigh." Only eldest sons got the honorary title and, of course, got to go first. This was the young man Cromwell might be usurping from his inheritance under a strict interpretation of the original settlement, Jane realized.

But that deed had gone up in flames, hadn't it?

It dawned on Jane that she hadn't actually checked but just taken Fitzwilliam's word for it. He could have found it convenient to make her think his dilemma had gone with the loss of the proof.

"Jane?" Deepti must have felt her pull away toward the house. "Aren't you going to watch?"

The papers could wait, but this might be Jane's only chance to see Arjun take on two young lords. "Will your father win?"

"Not if they are as good as they think they are," said Deepti enigmatically. From her tone, she didn't rate their skills as highly as they did.

Arjun bowed as Jamieson stepped into the ring. "My lord."

"So who's the dusky champion, Cromwell?" asked Jamieson. He rolled his shoulders and shook out his arms.

"My father's cook," said Cromwell, grinning.

"A cook? Let's see if I can make mincemeat of him then." And not waiting for further niceties, Jamieson lowered his head and went for Arjun like a battering ram taking a maharajah's castle by conquest – except he missed. Arjun had stepped aside at the last moment and his opponent had the indignity of hitting only the ropes. "Slippery little devil, isn't he?" Jamieson wiped his face on his shirtsleeve, failing to disguise his flush of anger.

"You're not the first to be caught out that way," said Cromwell easily. "The blacksmith's son hit the corner post in his bout."

Clearly not happy to be no better than a blacksmith's son, Jamieson turned. "Come here, you blighter. Stop dancing away from me."

"My father's advantage is speed and strength rather than weight," said Deepti in a low voice. "He will avoid being in a hold with a heavier man."

The two fighters circled, Arjun looking relaxed as if he had all the time in the world, Jamieson watching for an opening. Then the cook let his left shoulder drop a little.

"A bait," said Deepti. "And he takes it."

Jamieson charged Arjun, who moved fluidly sideways, grabbed the young lord, and tossed him over his hip. After an impressive tumble, Jamieson found himself on his back looking up at the sky.

Raleigh was quick to make fun of his brother's defeat. "Pathetic, Jamieson. Our old nanny could do better. Let me have a go."

"I've not finished," growled the lord, getting to his feet. His white shirt was now covered in grass stains.

"Then he'll take you both on!" said Cromwell. "Arjun, I'll double the prize money if you win. What say you to that?"

Deepti frowned. "That is too much, even for my father."

But Arjun clearly wanted the money more than he feared the risk of failure. "If my lord so wishes," he said.

"Both of us? Come now, Cromwell: he'll be cracked like an egg between us!" Raleigh gestured to their considerable bulk. "And I'm not as slow as Big Brother here."

"Oh? You don't think you'll win?" asked Cromwell lightly.

"I think we'll win too easily and maybe hurt your champion."

"Arjun, are you afraid?"

"No, sir."

Cromwell turned back to the Withers boys. "Then, my lords, I don't see the problem."

Raleigh shrugged. "Remember, this was your idea."

Chapter 31

Jane touched Deepti's arm. "Do you want me to attempt to stop this? I could ask Miss Felix."

Deepti bit her lip, then shook her head. "My father knows what he is doing – usually."

The numbers watching the match swelled as word spread that Arjun was taking on two young gentlemen.

"What's all this nonsense?" asked Sir Charles, arriving with Viscountess Felix and a man who, from his fine dress and noble bearing, Jane guessed to be Lord Withers.

"Lord Jamieson and Raleigh have challenged our champion," said Cromwell, eyes bright with excitement. "He's unbeaten so far today. You have no objection, my lord?" He deferred to the young men's father.

"It doesn't seem a very equal match but if they are content, I am too." Lord Withers was a surprise; a friendly looking man, Jane decided: kind brown eyes and a mass of black hair, not at all what she was expecting from the person who refused to speak to Sophias.

With a formal handshake, the combatants separated into three points of a triangle. Jane didn't think Arjun looked so confident anymore, perhaps regretting his agreement. It was too late now to back out. The Withers boys were watching each other. Jamieson pointed upward. Jane couldn't tell if that meant he was going for a high tackle, or telling his brother to do so. Clearly, this wasn't the first time they'd fought together.

And then, in a blink, it was all over.

Arjun didn't wait. While they were still strategizing, he ran forward and tackled Raleigh around the knees, tossing him over his back. He then swung around and dumped the young man on his brother so that they both ended up on the ground.

"Bravo!" cried Jane. So efficiently and elegantly done.

Raleigh got up. "Not fair. I wasn't ready."

"A bodyguard always has to be ready," murmured Deepti to Jane. "To save your princes, you have to end the fight before it really begins."

"Come now, lad, the man won fair and square," said Lord Withers. "Take the lesson that you aren't to judge a book by its cover. The man deserves his prize – and I'll double it for the outstanding skill he showed. A most useful servant, Sir Charles."

The landowner was not looking so pleased. "Indeed, sir."

The Withers boys reluctantly shook hands with Arjun and then walked off with Cromwell towards the beer tent. They were scowling, while Cromwell looked as if the bout had been his favourite birthday treat.

Deepti was hopping from foot to foot with excitement.

"What?" asked Jane.

"I think we have enough now. With my winnings – if I win – and with Father's, we can bring our family here."

Jane touched her arm. "I'm so pleased – really pleased. I know from my own family how horrid it is to be apart."

Sir Charles had stayed behind the crowds and taken his cook to one side. Jane could hear furious words coming from him, including "Should've lost to them", "What will they think of me?", and "No regard for my reputation!".

"I think Sir Charles is a sore loser," Jane murmured as Deepti scowled at the landowner. But what had he lost? It was his man who had won, wasn't it?

But the upper classes had lost to a foreign servant – and Sir Charles took the slight personally, as he felt he would be blamed when word got out among the gossips.

Taking a seat in the shade, Jane sketched out in her notebook her next letter home while events were still fresh in her mind.

A Letter to Underline Matters Between Us

Dearest Cassandra,

I have so much to tell you but I have promised (quite against my character) to be discreet. There are so many mysteries at <u>Southmoor Abbey</u> but, rest assured, I am on <u>fire</u> to solve them. There are more stories here than <u>in</u> our father's <u>library</u>. I can only drop hints about it now – <u>indeed</u>, that is all. I am <u>lost</u> for words to describe what is going on here. Tempers are liable to go up <u>in flames</u> any moment. It is public knowledge, though, that Sir Charles's favourite horses went missing yesternight, so I can tell you about that. There is no <u>proof of</u> foul play by anyone in the household but suspicion is scattered far and wide. Who took them is <u>disputed</u>. Sir Charles blames the travellers who came to entertain us at Cromwell's splendid party today, but I doubt that is the case. I notice that in this household, senior servants, such as a certain horrible head groom, take no <u>ownership of</u> their mistakes, blaming a poor stableboy (and one I have appointed an honorary Austen), Luke Tilney. He has lived on the <u>estate</u> all his life but now Sir Charles wants him <u>gone</u>. Luke knows this place <u>inside</u> out but had nothing to do with the theft. It is a <u>job</u> to know who to blame.

Your loving sister,

Jane.

Chapter 32

Around mid-afternoon, Jane remembered with a gulp of horror that she hadn't checked with Lady Cromwell whether she was allowed to attend the party. She'd been enjoying herself far too much to recall the annoying fact that she was here with duties of her own.

"Oh, I'm going to be in so much trouble!" she announced abruptly as she and Deepti watched the acrobats form a teetering human pyramid. Her own welcome at the Abbey was as shaky as the tower, and not attending her duties might just bring it all tumbling down.

"What trouble is that, Jane?" asked Deepti.

"I should be with Lady Cromwell." Jane looked down at her third-best dress. It had not borne well its adventures in the wood. "I look like I have been dragged through a hedge backwards!" Which, to be fair, was an accurate description of what she had been up to. "Must run!"

With a quick squeeze of Deepti's hand, Jane dashed back to the house.

Parks was in the hallway. "Miss Austen, Lady Cromwell has been asking for you."

BLAST! thought Jane. "I'll go to her at once" is what she actually said, thinking to make a quick change in her bedroom first. "Where is she, Mr Parks?"

"On the terrace. I am about to take tea out to her."

"I don't suppose the tray includes some cakes – and maybe some biscuits?"

"Just a few – to settle her nerves," agreed Parks.

"Two ticks and I'll be there."

"I'll bring a plate for you."

Jane took the stairs two at a time. "I believe I might just have to marry you, Parks."

"The honour would be mine, Miss Austen, but Mrs Parks might object."

Chuckling, Jane hurried up a second flight and into her bedroom. Her choice of dresses was limited so she opted for her second-best with a quick splash of water on face and hands to wash away the worst of the grime. Her hair was hopeless, so she bundled that up in a topknot and secured it with a green ribbon. It would have to do.

Such had been her speed that she arrived with the tea tray.

"Jane, Jane, where have you been?" complained Lady Cromwell. "Muffin has been at the silks again."

Pulse still racing, Jane took a stool next to the lady's embroidery frame and peered into the basket.

Jane 2, Muffin 2.

"If I might suggest, my lady, perhaps I could fashion a cover for your basket, then Muffin wouldn't be able to get inside?"

"Oh, but she does so love to play!"

With a sigh, Jane drew out the yellow thread and began untangling it. *Jane 2, Muffin 3.*

"Where have you been all afternoon? You look flushed – not a becoming colour for you. I suppose you slept late?" said Lady Cromwell as Parks handed her a plate of cakes. "Sir Charles admitted he'd sent you out with your dog to look for his horses. I told him that you are *my* companion, not his. If anyone is to give you orders, it is me, but he was quite unrepentant."

Fortunately, Lady Cromwell's thoughts were sent in another direction, as they had visitors.

"Mother! Have you greeted Lord Jamieson and Raleigh yet?" called Cromwell, coming up through the garden.

"More tea – and another plate of cakes, Parks," said the lady. "My lord, Mr Raleigh, a pleasure to see you. My, how you've both grown since we last met!"

Just behind the three men were Annette and her mother, and following them, Sir Charles and Lord Withers. Fitzwilliam brought up the rear, as usual not quite sure of his welcome. Jane watched with amusement as Lord Withers did indeed manage to avoid exchanging a word with Lady Cromwell by giving her a deep bow from some distance.

Servants carried out more tables and chairs so that the solitary sewing session turned into a little party all of its own. Tea was poured, cups handed around, and the flower borders complimented. Then the conversation naturally went to the events of the night.

"I'm sure your horses will be found," said Lord Withers.

"I wish I could be so sanguine," said Sir Charles.

"I can't blame you for feeling despondent, Sir Charles. I hear you've also burned down the library," said Lord Jamieson in a tetchy tone.

Someone was still fretting from their humiliation in the wrestling ring, thought Jane, tucking the newly wound yellow silk back into the basket.

"It's hardly burned to the ground, Jamieson," said Cromwell, answering for his father. "A little damage, nothing we can't fix. Besides, no one read all those stuffy old volumes. Whoever set the fire did us all a favour, wouldn't you agree, Miss Felix?"

"You can't mean that, Mr Cromwell," said Annette. "I know how you love to make fun of me so I shall assume you are jesting."

"But a dangerous machine was left running in there," persisted Jamieson, keen to score his point over the junior branch of the family. "Father would never've allowed that on any of our estates, and nor would I."

"I blame the maker of the machine," said Sir Charles, grabbing a coconut macaroon from the silver stand and stuffing it into his mouth whole. "It shows what happens when the lower classes bite off more than they can chew. I'm just sorry that I put up with the boy's nonsense for so long. Once this party is over, I'll make sure he knows his place."

"Others on your staff appear to have trouble with that concept too," said Lord Jamieson. He pointed at Jane, who was caught in the act of sliding a cake onto her plate.

Chapter 33

"My lord?" said Jane, blushing.

"You mean her?" Sir Charles scowled at Jane as he usually did when recalling her existence. "Oh, she's not a servant. She's the daughter of one of the local clergymen. I brought her here to keep my wife company for the week. Quite respectable, I assure you. A young lady, of sorts."

A leaf chose this moment to fall from Jane's hair on to her lap. Squirming inside with humiliation, Jane kept her smile fixed, rose, and bobbed a curtsey. "My lords."

Forced to acknowledge her now, the Withers boys gave her brief bows. Jamieson looked annoyed that his second dig at the family had gone wrong.

Their father, though, was more gracious, possibly to make up for his sons' lack. "And how are you enjoying your stay at Southmoor Abbey, Miss...?"

"Austen, Jane Austen," she said in defiance of the scorn poured on her plain name. "So far my visit has been very exciting. I've particularly enjoyed hearing about the history of the Abbey." Lady Cromwell and Fitzwilliam both gave her aghast looks. It would serve the Cromwells right if she did say something. "Have you heard of the legend of the Mad Monk?"

"Oh yes, that's a splendid tale," said Lord Withers. "Our ancestor

142

did him in, they say, and he haunts all of our blood ever since. I should watch out for him tonight in case he has designs on me – you too, boys, keep away from him if you want to live." He said it in such a cheerful tone it was clear he wasn't taking the threat seriously.

"I've seen no firm evidence that there is a ghost, sir," said Jane. "I think it more likely people make up tales when they see strangers walking about the grounds at night."

"I assure you the story is true, Miss Austen," said Sir Charles in a snippy tone. "The Abbey has an excellent ghost with a serious curse. I thank you for not voicing your ill-informed opinions on the subject again."

Sir Charles was a believer in the supernatural! Jane hadn't expected that. "Yes, sir."

"Ah-ha, Sir Charles! I see you are fierce in defence of the family legends. Quite so: such traditions have their place and add to the reputation of the Abbey. Such an old building without a decent ghost is surely unheard of in England, wouldn't you say, Lady Felix?" Lord Withers's eyes were twinkling.

"Oh yes. I'd get shot of any house of mine that couldn't summon up a spectre or two." Lady Felix and Lord Withers chuckled together. Sir Charles joined in, but a little late.

"But seriously, Sir Charles, might I see the damage done to the library?" said Lord Withers. "I believe it contains many important books and paintings belonging to my ancestors and I wish to reassure myself to their condition."

"*Our* ancestors," said Lady Cromwell. "They are mine as much as yours, my lord."

Lord Withers kept his gaze on Sir Charles.

"But of course, my lord. Whatever you wish," said Sir Charles.

"No time like the present," said Lord Withers, putting down his cup.

Jane was surprised when Lady Cromwell stood up. "I will show my cousins the library, Charles. The books were collected by my ancestors after all."

Jane followed the procession to the library. It appeared that everyone had decided to come along.

"Parks has done a good job clearing up, despite the other calls on the servants, what with the party and the ball," said Lady Cromwell. She didn't invite them to enter, but stood in the doorway and pointed to the singed patch. "There – not much to see. I believe it is almost time to dress for dinner? Shall we go up?"

Jane almost expected her to say "move along, ladies and gents, nothing to see here" like a Bow Street Runner dispersing a mob at the scene of a crime.

"Do you know what was lost?" asked Lord Withers, addressing Sir Charles.

"About fifty books, a table, and a Persian carpet that was worth more than the rest put together. I regret to say that we also lost some of the family archive – dashed nuisance that one. I've written to our solicitor to see if he has kept copies."

"The Cromwell archive – it was here?" Lord Withers's dark eyebrows were up in his fringe. "Good heavens, I had no idea you had that!"

"My wife had tasked Fitzwilliam with compiling a history for my son – a present for his birthday, though damned if I know if he'll ever read it. He is all for the future, my son, shows no interest in the past."

"A history?" Lord Withers turned to Fitzwilliam. "Young man, I would very much like a copy, but, tell me, what did you discover?"

Jane saw the look that passed between Fitzwilliam and Lady Cromwell. Which way would Fitzwilliam go now he was put on the spot?

"I… er… found a lot of very interesting material, my lord," said Fitzwilliam.

"About the Mad Monk?" Lord Withers sought out Jane in the crowd and gave her a wink.

Lord Withers was officially a GOOD EGG.

"Oh yes, about Abbot Roderick."

"Excellent. Perhaps you can read us that extract tonight, as long as it doesn't give the ladies nightmares?"

"Not likely," mumbled Jane.

"What about us poor sensitive gentlemen?" said Cromwell, feigning a swoon into Annette's arms.

"Oh, you silly creature!" she said, amused. "If ancient old ghost stories give you nightmares, then I'm the President of America."

Cromwell seized and kissed the back of her hand. "Madam President."

Much laughter followed that little byplay but Lord Withers hadn't forgotten his point. "And what else of interest have you found out, Fitzwilliam?"

The young man tugged at his cravat. Was he going to speak, wondered Jane, now in front of all these witnesses?

"Fitzbilly, find something interesting? I doubt it very much," said Cromwell to Lord Jamieson and Raleigh. "Born killjoy, that one."

Fitzwilliam shot him a furious look. Would that be enough to push him over the edge?

"I found many things that surprised me –" Fitzwilliam continued.

"And he's written all about them in his book," cut in Lady Cromwell. "Now I really must insist we all go up to get ready for dinner."

"Surprises?" asked Lord Withers.

"Yes, sir. But I didn't have time to authenticate them before the fire," said Fitzwilliam.

Lord Withers was no fool. "So they were to do with the family papers? Interesting. You must tell me more."

"Fitzwilliam, you are quite a disgrace in your wrinkled shirt. Go and change at once!" said Lady Cromwell.

Given a direct order, Fitzwilliam could not refuse. "Yes, my lady. My lord?"

"Yes, yes, do as the lady says. We'll continue our discussion later. Tomorrow perhaps?"

"I'm at your disposal, my lord." Fitzwilliam bowed to Lord Withers and headed to his room.

Lady Cromwell watched him go with a worried frown. She then turned to Sir Charles, who remained, while others drifted away to change.

"Charles, a word, please?"

"Really, my dear, now? I'm awfully busy." He got out a gold pocket watch and checked the time. "I wish to see what news the search party has for me. They are due to bring my hourly report."

"Yes, now." She folded her arms. "Charles, I mean it."

"Very well, my dear."

"And you, Jane. Run along now. I've asked my maid to lay out another dress for you. We can't have you appearing in the same one as last night, can we? What would our guests think?"

That Jane was as poor as a church mouse.

"Thank you, my lady." Jane bobbed a curtsey and headed upstairs, the blow of not being able to eavesdrop lessened by the prospect of a new gown. Such a rare event she felt it worth immortalizing in her notebook.

HAMPSHIRE TIMES

Country News *by Mr Bert Grubstreet*

SOUTHMOOR ABBEY COURT CIRCULAR

At the court of Sir Charles and Lady Cromwell, on this day, 26th June, 1789,

PRESENT

Among lords and ladies too numerous to mention was also the Right Honourable (in her own estimation) Jane Austen. The undistinguished guest appeared at dinner in a new gown, which the presiding queen of this court was happy to bestow upon her with all due pomp and circumstance (i.e. it was dumped on her bed). The said patriotic gown was sprigged with *fleur de lis* (lily petals to you and me) and in royal blue so a more loyal dress could not be found in the kingdom. Her attire was given as much praise as expected at dinner (none) and ended the evening hanging in splendour in the closet, having usurped Miss Austen's best gown from its throne.

Her old best is now her second-best.

The second-best is hereby demoted to its former place of third.

The third is restored to fourth.

Long live the king!

Chapter 34

With all hands now employed in preparing for the ball, Jane anticipated a quieter day than the tumultuous one of the tenants' party. This proved a very wrong assumption. A hurried tap came at her door at five-thirty in the morning. She opened it a crack to find Luke there.

LUKE!

"What are you doing in the house?" she asked. He would get into serious trouble if anyone spotted him indoors – and outside her room, no less.

"Miss Jane, you have to come!" he whispered, clearly so frantic that he didn't care about consequences.

"What's wrong? Is it Grandison?" Jane splashed a little cold water on her face to drive out the last remnants of sleep.

"No, no, it's Mr Fitzwilliam!"

What could have happened to him? Jane pulled her fourth-best dress over her nightgown and thrust her feet into her boots. "Come where?"

"To the stables. Oh, Miss, please hurry! He's to be taken to Winchester."

"Why there?"

"Sir Charles is the local magistrate. He's used his powers to arrest Mr Fitzwilliam on suspicion of arson and theft! Mr Fitzwilliam is to stay in gaol until his trial!"

Jane's fingers froze over her buttons. "No, that can't be right." Had she been that wrong about Fitzwilliam? Had he been hiding such wicked plots behind a pleasant face?

"Sir Charles swears he has proof. Please, Miss, you've got to come before they take him."

She grabbed a bonnet as a last-minute nod to propriety and tied it over her messy hair. "I'm ready."

They ran together to the stables, Jane aware of a stitch in her side, but she had no patience with such minor discomforts. Grandison came halfway and greeted them with agitated barks.

"Easy, boy," said Jane, not feeling the least bit easy herself.

They found Fitzwilliam standing between two gaolers about to climb on the back of a cart. A light rain was falling, plastering his dark curls to his scalp. His utter dejection was plain as his hands were manacled together and he was barely dressed, shirt open-collared with no cravat. He looked like he'd been pulled from his bed. A man who Jane deduced was his father also stood in the yard, propped up on his crutches, and clad in his nightgown. He was pleading with the men.

"My boy is innocent, I tell you!" said the steward. He was an older, more grizzled version of his son.

"In which case, sir, it will all come out at the trial, won't it?" said one of the gaolers in even tones.

"What evidence is there against him?" Jane asked briskly, keeping a grip on Grandison's collar.

"And who are you?" asked the gaoler, gaping at her like a stranded fish.

"A friend of the Cromwell family, and sister of the heir to the Knights of Godmersham Park," she said stoutly, drawing on her most impressive connections. "I asked a question. I expect an answer."

The gaoler clearly didn't know what to make of this self-confident young lady with a growling dog. "Well, Miss, an oilcan used for the machine that started the fire was found in the prisoner's private rooms, as well as a bag containing twenty guineas – proceeds, Sir Charles believes, from the sale of the stolen horses."

"There was no oilcan in my room – and those are my savings!" protested Fitzwilliam, but he might as well have been talking to a brick wall.

"We're taking him in, and, if he knows what's good for him, he'll confess what he did with them there horses," continued the gaoler. "He might avoid the noose if Sir Charles gets them back. You hear that, sir? Tell your son to make a clean breast of it and things might not go so badly for him."

"Edward!" The steward swayed. Luke slipped alongside him and held his elbow to steady him and led him over to a straw bale to sit.

"Pa, I'm innocent," called Fitzwilliam.

"I know, Edward." The steward straightened his bowed back. "My son has done nothing but show loyalty to a family that throws him away as soon as he becomes inconvenient to them!"

"Then he resents them, you'd say? Well, that gives him a good motive, don't it? Get up there, prisoner. Sir Charles wants us gone before his guests are stirring." The gaoler cracked his knuckles and then boosted Fitzwilliam on to the back of the cart, where the young man sat on the bare planks with head hung low.

"None of this is true," Fitzwilliam said in despair. He raised his gaze and met Jane's eyes. "You know what's really going on, don't you, Miss Austen? You know who wants me gone?"

Jane nodded. She had a suspicion that Sir Charles and Lady Cromwell were moving heaven and earth to stop Fitzwilliam talking to Lord Withers, going so far as to invent an accusation against him. But did they intend to silence him permanently by making him take the fall for a crime he did not commit?

"We'll help you, sir!" called Luke. "Don't you worry: we'll find out the truth."

Fitzwilliam gave him a weak smile. "Thank you, Luke. I'll remember you stood with me."

"Walk on," said the carter, flicking his whip over the sleepy head of his horse. The cart pulled out of the yard. Jane could do nothing to stop her friend being taken to gaol.

Chapter 35

Once the rattling died down and the devastated steward staggered back to his home, Luke turned to Jane, eyes afire. "Miss Jane, what are we going to do?"

Jane had never felt more powerless in her life. This was worse than flying from the front seat of George Watson's carriage. "I don't know."

"You've got to think of something! You're the clever one – you're always poking and prying and seeing things that others don't. You must've written something down in that little book of yours that can help us."

Jane felt ashamed that her notes were full of little jokes and stories for her sister – nothing that amounted to evidence to outweigh Sir Charles's trumped-up accusation. She'd been enjoying her own cleverness too much and now she felt a fool, two steps behind the perpetrators of these crimes at every stage. "I'm sorry, Luke; I haven't discovered anything that can contradict the evidence found in Fitzwilliam's room."

Luke waved her words away as if that were obvious. "I'm not expecting a miracle, but you've been on the right lines all along. Work out who took the horses, and you'll find the horses themselves. If we do that, the case against Mr Fitzwilliam collapses. Today! We've got to find them today!"

Luke was right. There was no other way of contradicting the authority of the landowner.

Grandison whined. He went to the archway, watching the cricket ball owner being taken away from him, then came back to Jane with his ears drooping. The poor dog looked as bereft as Jane felt.

Jane shook herself. Luke was showing more gumption than she and an Austen never cried "I give up!", not while they had breath in their body. "You're right. We need to follow up what we learned yesterday."

Luke scratched Grandison between the ears to set his tail wagging at half of its usual speed. "You said you had people to talk to at the party. Did they tell you anything?"

"Only that I'd been mistaken to suspect them."

"But clearing people helps. Let's go through it again. It's not you or me, not Mr Fitzwilliam…"

"Not Deepti and Arjun."

Luke raised his brows at this, but didn't ask why her suspicions had gone that way. "Not Lord Withers and sons, as they arrived after."

Organizing what they knew would help her think more clearly. Jane took out her notebook and sat on the edge of a trough to make a list. "The other guests and Sir Charles and Lady Cromwell were in their bedrooms when the fire broke out, so they are unlikely to have been outside stealing horses. I saw Parks too. I'm afraid I can't name all the other servants but I know some of the faces. It looked like most of the footmen were there and the maids were in the yard filling buckets. A little bit later I saw Cromwell and Fitzwilliam carrying out a carpet."

Luke leaped on that hint. "But not earlier? I saw Mr Cromwell coming in from the garden with flowers in his hair. Maybe that was to disguise his real purpose? Maybe he hadn't been celebrating with the travellers but just come from taking the horses to the cottage, leaving them there until he could go back to move them later?"

The timing did fit. "But why steal something that belongs to your own family?"

Luke scrunched up his nose in thought. "I reckon it's because his father was never going to give him Arachne. Sir Charles has made no secret of how little love he has for his son, not like his horses. Mr Cromwell must've got sick of it. Maybe to spite Sir Charles, he took the two things that his father loves most. He might not even intend to sell them – maybe he just wants to be the hero that finds them to earn his father's good opinion?"

"Then surely he won't let this situation go on much longer? He won't want his childhood friend imprisoned for something he didn't do." At least, Jane hoped not. If Lady Cromwell had told her son about what Fitzwilliam had found in the archive, and that he was the only one to have read the deed, then Cromwell might be pleased to see the obstacle removed. A felon would not be able to bear witness to what he found in the now incinerated papers – a neat solution to their problems.

While Jane and Luke were deliberating over their list, Sir Charles strode into the yard, Scroop at his heels.

"Scroop, ring the bell! Get those lazy blighters down here," ordered Sir Charles. His eyes fell on Jane. "What are you doing here?"

She was caught.

Chapter 36

J ane slipped the notebook away just as Grandison dropped a stick at her feet – correction, not a stick but a much-chewed whip. "I came to check on my dog."

"At six in the morning?"

"I'm an early riser."

"Humph! Get back to the house. I don't want you out and about until Fitzwilliam's partners-in-crime are caught. I couldn't face your father if something happened to you while in my care."

Now he worried about her safety!

"Sir." Jane bobbed a curtsey, gave Luke a look that promised they would speak later, and headed out of the stables. She didn't go far, only so as to be out of sight. Circling around to an open door, she waited to see what had brought Sir Charles to the stables.

The ringing bell summoned the grooms and boys to the yard. They came from their sleeping quarters, hitching up their breeches, rubbing at tired eyes, scratching unshaven jaws.

"You can probably guess why I've brought you together," said Sir Charles.

None of them looked as though they had the least clue.

"Arachne and Romeo were the crown jewels of this stable and you lost them. Southmoor Abbey will now never be home to the premier breeding stock of Hampshire – my dream is at an end."

Awkward feet shuffled. Caps were squeezed between work-worn fingers.

"It seems increasingly likely that the thieves were from this estate, led by Edward Fitzwilliam." That brought a very surprised reaction from those gathered. "Some of you, I realize now, had to have been helping him – and I promise you I'll prove this and you'll pay dearly. But that leaves me with a pressing problem. I cannot have my remaining horses cared for by men I do not trust. So I have decided that I must start again. You are all, apart from Scroop, to be let go on Monday."

Jane heard the gasp from all gathered.

"I know that the innocent are being made to suffer by the guilty, but that's the way of the world. I make no apology for putting my horses first. You can pick up your wages from Scroop Monday morning and I expect you all to be off my land by midday."

"But, sir!" said one elderly man, the one with the limp Jane had seen cleaning the cobbles. "Where are we to go?"

"It's high summer, almost harvest: there's work aplenty on the farms hereabout. If the guilty are identified, then you are welcome to reapply for your old jobs. That's all I have to say on the matter. Good day to you all."

Jane realized that, announcement over, Sir Charles was heading back to the house and would spot her if she stayed where she was. Taking a leap over the fence into a herb garden, she dived behind a low box hedge, lying flat on the gravel, and prayed he wouldn't peer over the top to find her sprawled there. Footsteps scrunched by but, as there was no cry of outrage, it appeared she had gone undetected.

Once she judged it safe, Jane picked herself up and brushed off her skirt. Sir Charles was very quick to get rid of his staff. He showed no mercy, like a man lopping off an infected wound without giving it a chance to heal. The reaction was extreme and out of proportion.

And if Sir Charles knew, as Jane suspected, that Fitzwilliam was innocent...

Chapter 87

Unfortunately, the investigation had to be put aside for a few hours. Jane boiled with frustration when she discovered that Lady Cromwell required her attendance all that afternoon to help trim her ballgown with a new length of Brussels lace. If Jane had been the suspicious type (which she was), she would've suspected that this was on purpose to stop her asking questions of the servants about how the oilcan came to be found in Fitzwilliam's room. Jane plied her needle as fast as she could, hoping for early release, but that meant Lady Cromwell merely found new tasks for her.

"Oh my, Jane, you have a very neat stitch!" Lady Cromwell said admiringly – the first compliment she had paid her companion. "I did not suspect what talents you were hiding under your unremarkable appearance." Lady Cromwell snipped a length of scarlet silk and threaded her needle. "I know you might think it odd that I can go ahead and dance the night away when a young man – one who was like a son to me – lies in gaol, but I tell you, it is the only way I can support the thought that we have been so deceived by him." She put down her embroidery frame, sniffed, and dabbed her dry eye with a handkerchief. "We cherished a viper at our breast."

"Surely it is not proven that he had anything to do with the horses? And the oilcan might have not been the same one."

"Oh, but it was. It had the stables mark on it. I'm afraid it is all quite settled: Fitzwilliam was all this time plotting against us to spoil Wicky's big day. He was jealous, you see."

Jane did not see, but held her tongue.

"And he wanted to get away, go back to university. He decided stealing was the only path open to him."

Jane had to bite her tongue this time, as she had been present but two days ago when Lady Cromwell had promised to see that Fitzwilliam resumed his university education. He had no need to take desperate measures – and they both knew it.

"You understand that, don't you, Jane? This is what happened?"

Just saying something happened a certain way didn't make it true. Jane dropped her needle so she wouldn't have to reply. She patted down the billowing yellow silk to find it.

"Jane?"

"There it is!" Jane produced the needle. "Almost done, my lady. You'll look splendid tonight, far too young to be the mother of a young man coming of age."

The flattery successfully diverted Lady Cromwell from the talk that Jane suspected Sir Charles had asked her to have with her companion.

"You think so?" asked the lady, looking at her reflection in the back of a teaspoon. "You don't think I show the strain of the last few days?"

There were indeed signs that Lady Cromwell hadn't been sleeping. "No one would dare suggest such a thing," Jane said truthfully. "I've finished." She snapped off the thread. "May I be excused? I need to retire for a moment."

"I want you back here immediately. Lady Felix and her daughter are joining me for a hand of cards and we need a fourth."

Jane bobbed a curtsey and walked swiftly away before even this concession was withdrawn. She ducked back into the adjacent morning room, found a desk, and took out a sheet of paper, which she divided into two. The Cromwells seemed set on keeping her out of the way until the ball, but then they would have other things on their minds. Jane needed help to return to her search. She'd had some new ideas while sewing the lace on the bodice of the gown. Lady Cromwell had had it let out to accommodate the extra pounds she had gained over the last week and the lace was to hide the old seam. That put Jane in mind of the ways appearances can be altered, traces concealed. Building on Luke's idea, a new theory was taking shape, one that went back to the very first mystery she had come to solve.

However, she needed reinforcements to find proof. Quickly, she scrawled a note to Deepti and Luke, begging them to meet her in the kitchen courtyard with lanterns once the ball was underway.

They had a mad monk to confront.

Chapter 38

Lady Cromwell sent Jane off for an early night after the ladies retired from the dinner table.

"You are too young to attend such an event as the ball," Lady Cromwell told her. "And, besides, I'm sure you don't have anything suitable to wear."

Jane had a donated gown that would pass well enough in Steventon, but Lady Cromwell was probably right that it would make her an object of mockery in this much more exulted company. Every carriage that came down the drive was delivering a baronet, or marchioness, or, at the very least, a squire. Besides, she had made alternative, much more exciting, plans for her evening.

"Certainly, I shall go up. I hope you have a lovely time," Jane said coolly.

"Thank you, Jane. And tomorrow I'll write to your mother – tell her to expect you home… shall we say Wednesday? I'll ask Cromwell to see you to the inn. You'll be met, I trust?"

Young ladies did not travel on the public stagecoach alone. "If we give my parents warning, that can be arranged," Jane said. The Cromwells wanted rid of her as soon as possible; she had become an awkward witness to their behaviour, as Fitzwilliam had warned her during their very first conversation.

"Good girl. Now run along upstairs." Lady Cromwell was pleased by Jane's lack of argument, mistaking this for obedience. "You can watch from the library window later if you like. You won't bother anyone from there."

Jane changed into her poor old fourth-best gown. It had taken so much rough treatment and Jane suspected more of the same was in store tonight.

"You aren't going to the ball?" said Parks, meeting her outside the library. He was carrying away a tray of post-dinner drinks and cigars, sign that the gentlemen had gone up to dress. "I thought that you would be invited?"

Jane shook her head. "Not old enough, Mr Parks. I'm not officially out yet. I can go to parties at home but not in high society like this."

"Ah, of course, I was forgetting. Is there anything I can get you, Miss Jane?"

"I'm sure you have your hands full, Mr Parks. I'll come down to the kitchen for supper later." And there she provided herself with an excuse to roam if he should see her.

"Very good, Miss." He turned to the servants' staircase.

"And Mr Parks?"

"Yes, Miss?"

"About that oilcan?"

"Ah." He glanced about, checking no one was listening. "The maid who cleans Master Fitzwilliam's rooms swears it wasn't there before yesterday, but it was found hidden under the bed when Sir Charles ordered a search late last night, so she may just have missed it."

It was awfully convenient for Sir Charles to have the sudden whim to check on the steward's son's bedchamber and no other room. "Who keeps an oilcan under their bed?"

"Someone wanting to conceal what they did."

Or someone who wanted to frame another person for their own crime by putting it in a place Fitzwilliam wouldn't immediately notice. "I don't think Mr Fitzwilliam had anything to do with the theft or the fire."

"I hope you're right, Miss. It will kill his father if he goes to the gallows." With a nod, Parks headed at a brisk pace to greet the arrivals.

It was too soon to go down to meet her friends so Jane took up Lady Cromwell's suggestion to watch the arrivals from the library. First, she examined the ruined shelf more closely, something she hadn't yet had time to do. The worst damage had been done on the bottom rows, just where "Cr" would be filed. In fact, now that she looked more carefully, there were signs that burning oil had been splashed deliberately on this section of shelving. There were greasy patches on the floorboards nearby that hadn't caught fire.

She sat back on her heels. This was proof the fire had been set deliberately to destroy the inheritance deed. As far as she knew, the only people to know the papers existed were Fitzwilliam, Lady Cromwell, and herself. How could the knowledge have spread? Fitzwilliam might've told someone, it was true, but Jane thought it was more likely he was still agonizing over what to do with his dangerous knowledge. He might've told his father, but she couldn't imagine him framing his own son for the fire. No, that was implausible in the extreme. That left Lady Cromwell. Either she set the fire herself, or told someone else and they did so. The most likely candidates were, naturally, her husband or her son.

Three suspects – and Jane had no clue how to find out which one did it. Maybe they were all in on it? They all stood to benefit from keeping the estate.

The sound of an orchestra tuning up took Jane from the floor to the window overlooking the lawn and the illuminated ruins. A perfect summer evening was unfolding as the sun set. Flocks of young ladies moved across the lawn, trying to attract the attention of a desirable partner. The gentlemen stood around the edges of the dance floor, avoiding the eyes of match-making mamas. Jane spotted Annette standing apart from the other girls. Her dress was an unflattering mustard colour, which Jane suspected had been chosen on purpose to deter male attention. She had her head angled away from the orchestra and the first couples taking a turn on the springy grass. It was the stance of someone looking for a particular person. Cromwell? No, he was dancing with a girl in a pink dress.

Lord Withers appeared, ushering his two boys in the direction of the unpartnered girls, a shepherd sending his sheepdogs to do their duty. Annette made straight for him.

Lord Withers? Jane guessed by the absence of a Lady Withers that he was a widower, but wasn't he far too old for Annette?

The lady exchanged brief greetings, then said something which had Lord Withers drawing her aside. They stood close together by a stone fountain topped by Cupid, out of the general mêlée. Whatever Annette had to say was clearly fascinating, far more interesting than the arrow aimed by Cupid at the lord's back.

Chapter 39

J ane blew out a breath. *BOTHER.* She was much too far away to make even a decent guess at lip-reading.

Jane waited until all the Cromwells and guests were present before making her way down to the kitchen. Arjun was busy icing little cakes so didn't notice her pass. Luke and Deepti were waiting for her in the courtyard, eyeing each other a little distrustfully.

"Oh, you don't know each other, do you?" said Jane brightly. Indoor and outdoor staff rarely met. "Luke, Deepti; Deepti, Luke."

"Why did you ask us to come to meet you, Jane?" asked Deepti.

"Luke and I are investigating the missing horses," Jane explained quickly. "We have to find them so we can prove that Fitzwilliam hasn't stolen them."

Deepti looked doubtful. "But won't the thieves be long gone?"

Jane shook her head. "I think not. Luke and I found where the horses were taken to start with – the old gamekeeper's cottage. Do you know it?"

"I think so – in the woods?"

"That's right. Luke says two horses were kept there briefly before being moved again."

"But they were moved further off, surely?"

"I don't think so. A full-scale search was underway once their disappearance was announced. If Luke is right, while the searchers were sent off far and wide, the horses were in fact moved closer where they could be looked after. The thief didn't want any harm to come to these valuable animals."

Luke's ears pricked up at that. "You agree that it was Cromwell?"

"I'm not certain but I think it very possible. What I am sure about is that this was long in the planning – that someone has been laying a false trail for weeks."

"Who?" asked Deepti.

"The Mad Monk."

Luke went white. "I'm not getting near no ghost!"

"Nor I!" said Deepti. "Everyone says you die if you see him!"

"Exactly!" Jane clapped her hands. "That's good!"

"How can that be good, Jane?"

"Because you are proof that everyone believes it – apart from Fitzwilliam, but he's been taken out of the picture for other reasons." They still looked confused. "Someone has been masquerading as the Abbey ghost for a while now to prepare the way for this little sleight of hand – a theft that wasn't a theft and a fire that, if I'm right, wasn't started by your machine, Luke." Jane walked to the canvas that had been thrown over the steam engine when it was dumped in the yard. She pulled it off. "Have a look. Tell us if there's any sign your model started that blaze."

Luke kneeled beside it, reassembling the jumbled pieces.

"It struck me that you'd built it with safety features – the whistle for one. I couldn't understand how it could have set fire so quickly to the shelf. Surely it would've had to explode at the very least? But it was still shrieking away when we reached the library, going like the clappers."

"That's true," agreed Deepti. "My father smothered it with a curtain while it was still turning and whistling."

Luke found the little firebox. It had buckled with the heat but was in one piece. "No explosion," he said. "I could mend this easily and it would work again. How did the fire begin then?"

"Oil," said Jane. "Find a can of lamp oil in the stables, pour it on the tablecloth, and leave a trail to the bookcase and light it with a candle. The machine was just to confuse us and stop too much damage being done. In a sense, it was our fire alarm. The person knew the whistle would sound. We were meant to hear it – meant to come and put out the flames before they took hold."

"But why?" asked Deepti. "To give them time to steal the horses?"

"If I'm right, I think the horses had already been stolen by then. No, this was because Fitzwilliam had found out something the Cromwells wanted kept hidden – something in that bookcase. I can't tell you what exactly as I've given a promise, but I can say that I'm convinced he's innocent, that one of the family did this, and that they'll see him hang rather than let the truth be known."

Luke and Deepti both looked grim-faced at this announcement.

Jane rubbed her hands. "So who is up for a little ghost-hunting?"

Chapter 40

"Fake ghost-hunting?" queried Deepti.

"Of course," said Jane firmly. "There's no such thing as ghosts."

"There is," said Luke.

"I haven't got time to argue this with you, Luke, but I promise in this case there isn't. Are you with me?" She put out her hand and waited for them to put theirs in hers so they made a pact. "It's agreed."

"Where are we going to look for the fake ghost and lost horses?" asked Deepti.

"The ruins: the one place we keep being told definitely not to go."

"I don't like this," muttered Luke.

"But you're brave enough to face your fears, aren't you?" said Jane in a bracing tone.

He looked at the two girls and nodded. "Aye. For Mr Fitzwilliam."

They carried their lanterns out into the tumbled-down Abbey. Jane needed to check on the progress of the ball to ensure they still had time to search, so passed her lantern to Deepti.

"I won't be a moment."

She crept to the edge of the chapel, keeping out of the coloured lantern-and-mirror illuminations. Fortunately, these also cast deeper shadows. She lay on her stomach to look through a gap. A second later she jumped as Deepti and Luke joined her, lanterns left behind.

Luke grinned nervously at her. "Partners, remember?"

"Shh!" warned Jane as the music died away and Sir Charles stood forward.

"My lords, ladies, and gentlemen, thank you so much for being with us tonight to help celebrate our dear son's coming-of-age." He threw an arm around Cromwell's shoulder and squeezed him tight. "Many of you will know that I had hoped to mark the occasion by making him a special present of a remarkable horse, but fate intervened." He looked sombre for a moment. "However, I don't want to disappoint my beloved boy on his special day. I have arranged another present that I know will be even more to his taste." Cromwell's expression was one of scepticism. "My son, I have arranged for you to go on the Grand Tour, starting in Paris next month, and from there you will be able to see all those places you often talk about – Switzerland, the Alps, Rome, even Greece if you wish. All your expenses will be covered. The only thing your mother and I ask is that you come back safely."

Cromwell gaped. "You are doing this – for me? Oh goodness, Father, that's so generous of you!"

"We don't always see eye to eye – what father and son do? But I want you to have your dream even if I can't have mine."

Lady Cromwell dabbed at her eyes. Jane wondered whether they were genuine tears of joy as her husband and son embraced and applause rang out.

"I think that's the cue for us to restart the music. My dear, will you dance with me?" Sir Charles bowed over his wife's hand.

Jane shuffled back to where they had left the lanterns. "Interesting" was all she would say when the others asked her what she thought of that.

"Does it help clear up who stole the horses?" asked Luke. "If it were Cromwell, surely now he'll want to repay his father by producing them and ending his misery?"

"You would think that, wouldn't you?" Jane set off for the parts of the ruins that remained in darkness. "We'll see."

Jane led them to the first of the locked storerooms she remembered from her early examinations of the ruins.

"You think the horses might be in here?" asked Deepti, rattling the padlock.

Jane shushed her. "There might be someone with them."

Luke put his head to the door. "Can't hear nothing – no man, no horses."

"Who has keys?" asked Jane in a low voice.

Deepti thought a moment. "One set is with Mr Parks and the other with Sir Charles."

Jane debated how far Parks's goodwill would bend toward her. He was a loyal family servant. Not as far as breaking into forbidden storerooms, she guessed.

"You don't need the key." Luke slipped a tool for removing stones from horses' hooves out of his boot. "This usually works." He jiggled it in the keyhole, twisted – and the padlock opened.

"Well done, Luke! You must teach me how to do that," Jane said enviously – another accomplishment she wished young ladies were taught. "Ready? Now!" She pulled open the door.

Chapter 41

"Oh."

An empty room stretched before them. A melted stub of an old candle showed it had been used once upon a time, but not for a while. There were mushrooms growing in the mould. A pile of grey rags was heaped in the nearest corner.

"It was a good thought," said Deepti.

"I thought this one was the most likely," said Jane, unable to hide her disappointment. "The rest are cellars, like the one I fell into."

"Then we'd better check everything – just to be thorough," said Luke. "The horses could've been here – like at the cottage." He poked at the rags. They rattled. "Jane!"

"I hear it!"

As he lifted up a filthy monk's habit stained with rusty blood, Jane pulled out a length of old chain.

"Believe me now?" she asked Luke.

He nodded. "I believe that someone has been pretending to be the ghost. That's so dangerous! What if the real ghost punishes them for it?"

Jane rolled her eyes, but behind his back where he couldn't see.

"It's not enough to prove Mr Fitzwilliam innocent, though, is it?" said Deepti.

"No, unfortunately, it's not enough, but it does seem as though we're on the right track," said Jane. "But where are the horses if not here? This was the best contender, as you can walk the horses right inside."

"And for that reason, Mr Parks would have checked," said Deepti. "He made a very complete search of the area around the house, including the ruins."

"We'd better look at the other storage cellars, just to be sure," said Jane.

Without much hope of finding the horses in the ruins now, they broke into the other two cellars that Jane had not yet been inside and found the same story: empty, with no sign of recent activity.

"I'm sorry," said Jane, slumping down on to a fallen stone. "I was so sure – what with the monk – the ban on going into the ruins – the locked storeroom: it all fitted so well together. It seemed just like something Mr Cromwell would do."

Music bounced up to the stars and down again as a lively country dance wove patterns on the ballroom lawn.

"It was a good plan. Someone should've thought of it," said Luke. "I guess the monk's habit might've been Mr Cromwell playing a joke when he was younger? Nothing to do with the horses?" He dug in his pocket, and then tossed a cricket ball hand to hand to help him think. "What now?"

Jane's eyes fixed on the ball. "Where did you get that?"

"The gaolers emptied Mr Fitzwilliam's pockets before putting on the cuffs. He told me to keep it for your dog – that was just before I came to get you."

Grandison… GRANDISON!

Jane leaped up. "Come on!"

Jane, you are a goose! she thought, shaking her head at herself. She had asked her dog to lead her to the nice horse that smelled of sugar, and he had brought her right here and bounced on the same trapdoor she'd fallen through. Jane had assumed he was playing, remembering his triumph of the previous morning, but what if…

"Does she do this often?" she heard Deepti ask, a few steps behind. "Take off like that without explaining?"

"I think so. It's something to do with being an Austen."

"English girls are odd."

"I have to agree."

"Quiet now!" Jane warned.

They crept toward the last trapdoor, the one she had dismissed, thinking the room below was too far down to stable a couple of horses. Her heart leaped in anticipation when she saw that the padlock was off once more. She gestured to Deepti to take one side, Luke the other, while she held her lantern high. On her nod, they lifted the door.

In the bottom of the pit, startled eyes looked up briefly, then darted away. Scroop, who had been sitting on a low stool, leaped to his feet and held a wooden cross in front of him, eyes screwed shut.

"Back, you fiend!"

The two missing horses were tethered either side of him. A wooden ramp, which had been hidden under the pile of earth Jane had fallen on, leaned up at a shallow angle to the entrance overhead, its surface muffled by old turnip sacks. The horses could travel up and down that with no risk to life or limb. In fact, in the summer with a bed of soft straw and their usual bag of oats, the horses would be quite comfortable. They even had a little lantern burning on the wall between them. Arachne didn't like the dark, Jane remembered.

Jane stood at the top of the ramp, blocking a quick departure. "Resorted to stealing horses, have you, Mr Scroop?"

"You!" said Scroop. He dropped his hand from his face. "You interfering little minx!" The groom stood up and grabbed a horsewhip. "These horses aren't stolen!"

"Thank you for confirming that," said Jane with a brisk nod. "I take it you're here on the orders of Mr Cromwell? How perfectly horrid of him." Cromwell must have been preparing the temporary stable in his disguise when she had the misfortune to fall in. He likely had never known she was there.

"How little you know!" scoffed Scroop. "That's a lie – and no one will believe you!" He shook the whip at her. "And if you dare speak a word about this, I'll make you sorry!"

"Your threat has witnesses." Jane hadn't really thought this part of the investigation through: what to do when confronting the guilty party.

He looked taken aback for a second until he saw it was only Deepti and Luke with her. "You think a Hindoo girl and a fatherless orphan will be believed over me? I'm Sir Charles's most trusted servant!"

"But Mr Fitzwilliam is wrongly accused of stealing these same horses! Surely you can't stand by and let him take the blame?"

"I surely can. Another do-gooder who poked around more than was good for him. Now run along, the three of you! There'll be hell to pay tomorrow when I tell Sir Charles what you've been up to!"

"But that's outrageous!" Jane could feel the rage bubbling up from her toes to the top of her head. "You're despicable!"

"No, I'm a very rich man, thanks to this. I'll get the credit for finding them, position secure for life. Just think, girl, what can you say? That you discovered the horses? Sir Charles won't like you blaming his son. And I'll just tell Sir Charles that I found *you* with them and that you've been helping Fitzwilliam all along. You'll all end up sitting alongside him in Winchester gaol!"

Chapter 42

Luke touched her arm. "Come along, Jane. He's right: we can't say anything. You might have family who will come for you in a few days – but I don't and Deepti's a foreigner. They'll suspect her just because she's an outsider."

Scroop nodded. "The lad knows the way of the world. Tootle off to bed now, Miss – and keep your trap shut."

Jane kicked the door down on him, drowning out his laughter. "I hate him!" But no Austen would let a man get away with this. She might be just a rector's daughter, but she could outwit the spoiled son of the house and his ruffian. Oh yes, this could be good – very good indeed. "I've an idea."

Luke looked to Deepti. "Why am I worried?"

"Because she is about to do something very peculiar," said Deepti soberly.

"Exactly! The only matter to settle is which one of us should do it," said Jane. They both pointed at her. "Oh, very well. You'll need to get one of the mirrors and something to make the sounds while I get dressed. Anyone got an empty bottle?"

Fifteen minutes later, the three were back by the trapdoor. Luke, who had relocated one of the large mirrors for the illuminations and positioned it as instructed, had kept watch. He assured them Scroop had not emerged. If the groom was going to tell tales on them to Sir Charles, he was waiting until the ball was over. Deepti had fetched two empty champagne bottles from the kitchen. That left Jane. She tripped as she hurried to rejoin them. The Mad Monk's habit was too long for her, and smelled terrible, but if this worked she wouldn't need to wear it for long.

"Are you sure Scroop doesn't know about the fake monk – that he'll be scared?" whispered Deepti.

"Did you see his reaction when we first opened the trapdoor?" said Jane. "He, like everyone here, sincerely believes there's a ghost –"

"There is," said Luke.

"Well, for our purposes, let's hope his superstition is running as strong as yours." Jane got into position. "Is here right?" She glided across the soft turf. Luke lay on his stomach to check the angle and gave her a thumbs up. "Let's do this."

Deepti hid herself behind a nearby wall, blowing gently in the bottles to make a mournful wailing noise. After a few unsettling minutes of ghostly noises, Luke eased up the trapdoor, keeping out of sight of Scroop.

"Back again, are you?" growled the groom. "I'll beat you, I will, and hang the consequences!" He paused, and his tone changed. "What's that noise?"

That was perfect: Scroop was coming out. As he climbed the slope, Jane flipped up the deep hood and walked with monastic grandeur across the Abbey ruins, lit only by a lantern. Scroop couldn't see her directly, but he would be able to watch her progress in the reflection of the large mirror. It would look to him as if the Mad Monk were floating above the ground, flying over the monks' graveyard. Deepti rattled the chain.

"The ghost! Oh my eyes, I've seen the ghost!" Scroop choked. His gratifying panic attack did the rest of the work for them. With a strangled cry, Scroop stumbled off for the house, calling for help.

As soon as he quit the field, Jane wriggled out of the habit and dumped it behind the nearest gravestone. "Quick! We don't have long!"

Luke was already in the cellar, crooning to the horses. The next part of the plan was hampered by the fact there were only leading reins and no saddle in the temporary stable.

"Luke," Jane said as she held Arachne for him so he could bring out Romeo, "can you ride without a saddle?"

"Of course." He shrugged as if that was obvious.

"I can too," said Deepti.

"Oh, you really are the most splendid partners a girl could ask for! Don't tell me, your father's been teaching you?"

Deepti nodded. "Can't every rider manage without – in case you have to make a quick escape?"

"Absolutely not," said Jane, thinking of the performance she had to go through to get on the back of a horse: mounting block, side-saddle, riding habit… "Remember: don't let anyone stop you. Ride straight to the middle of the dance floor and I'll catch up."

"Er, Deepti, the mare has never been ridden," cautioned Luke.

Deepti swung on Arachne's back, gripping hard with her knees when the horse danced under the unaccustomed weight. Leaning forward, she whispered something in the mare's ears and Arachne settled.

Deepti patted the mare's neck. "Do not worry, Luke. She's a good horse."

"And you're a good rider," he said with a grin.

"Let's go!" Deepti tapped Arachne's flanks with her heels and the mare broke into a trot. Luke followed. Jane had to jog, then run flat out to keep up. They rode right through the chapel and out what had been the north door. This took them across the drive and down on to the ballroom lawn.

But no one was looking! The orchestra was playing too loudly, and the guests were too absorbed in their own affairs to notice what was approaching fast from the ruins.

Then Deepti let out a wild cry – Jane felt it might have been the sound her ancestors made as they rode into battle. Luke joined in with a "tally ho!". Jane added her piercing whistle. Dancers scattered. The two horses circled in the centre of the dance floor, Jane but seconds behind.

The orchestra ground to a halt.

"What is all this?" asked Sir Charles. "This is an outrage!"

Cromwell stood on the dance floor with Annette in his arms, his expression one of utter amazement. "The horses – they're back!" he said.

And that was when Jane realized she'd read the clues all wrong.

Chapter 48

J ane climbed on the conductor's box, displacing the musician with a brief apology. "My lords, ladies, and gentlemen," she said, tapping the music stand to gain their attention. "Please forgive the interruption, but we wanted to return the missing horses as soon as possible to their rightful owners."

"They were hidden close," said Luke from Romeo's back, pointing to the illuminated chapel. "In the ruins. We found them just now."

"Mr Scroop, the head groom, was with them," added Deepti. "But he ran off."

"Scroop?" asked Cromwell. "*He* stole them?"

"No, sir," said Jane. "Scroop was just following orders. These horses were never stolen; it was just arranged to look as though they had been."

"Nonsense!" barked Sir Charles. "The guilty man is in Winchester gaol. Girl, you are quite out of line. Get down from there!"

"No, I won't. The guilty man is here – not in gaol. The horses were first taken by Scroop from the stable to be hidden in the woods while he kept everyone else busy."

"Ridiculous!" fumed Sir Charles.

"Then he moved them to the ruins, but only after they'd been checked by the butler. This was done during a purposely chaotic search where clues were trampled, and tracks hidden."

"Girl, your father will hear of this!"

"There's more. The one who ordered their removal wanted them kept safe – and close, so he could check on them as he loves them dearly. There never were any thieves – but then you knew that all along, didn't you, Sir Charles?"

"Father?" asked Cromwell. "Did you do this so you didn't have to give me Arachne?"

Sir Charles opened his mouth.

"There's no point denying it. Scroop doesn't have an ounce of courage: he'll tell all if he faces prosecution for horse-thieving."

"It was all a trick – a jest!" cried Sir Charles, changing tack. "Ha-ha-ha!"

No one else joined in his laughter.

"Sir Charles, what have you done?" asked Lord Withers. "An innocent man has been sent to prison on your orders! Why?"

"You could've just told me that you'd prefer to pay for my Grand Tour. I'd've taken that over a horse," said Cromwell.

"Your mother made me promise," grumbled Sir Charles. It was finally dawning on him that he was being disgraced in front of everyone who was anyone in Hampshire high society.

"But why turn on your protégé?" persisted Lord Withers.

"Because he found out something they didn't want to come to your attention," said Jane, deciding that their treatment of Fitzwilliam put an end to her promise of silence. "A deed concerning the inheritance of the Abbey, which someone tried to destroy in the library fire. That's why Lady Cromwell didn't make more of a protest when Mr Fitzwilliam was arrested."

"Me?" Lady Cromwell fluttered her fan.

"It wasn't my model that set your library on fire, Sir Charles," said Luke.

"Yes, it was!" countered Sir Charles.

"No. The evidence is still here, by the kitchen door. My engine is barely damaged, with no signs any part of it caught alight."

"The engine actually saved us all," added Jane, "as it raised the alarm. You should thank him."

That lit the gunpowder that was Sir Charles's temper. "Thank him! Thank a servant's whelp! And I suppose you want thanks too? You, a headstrong clergyman's daughter from an obscure parish – one who has clearly been reading far too many novels and filled her head with foolishness!"

"There's nothing wrong with novel-reading." But Jane knew she was getting off the point.

"There's no proof of any of this," said Lady Cromwell.

"I'm afraid there is," said a new voice.

Chapter 44

It wasn't Jane who spoke, but Annette. "On my first night here, I took some books from the library. I was interested in how the Abbey came to the Withers family so I removed the volume in which the legal papers were bound – wills, land deeds, important letters. It would've been lost in the fire but instead it was in my room. I didn't realize the significance until I heard Mr Fitzwilliam mention to Lord Withers that he had found some interesting documents he had not had time to authenticate. And then he was arrested, which made me wonder. I spent the day reading the papers, as I told Lord Withers earlier." She turned to Cromwell. "I'm sorry."

"Sorry?" Cromwell pulled a wry face. "I suppose it was too much to expect we could get away with it, wasn't it, Mama?"

"Wickham Cromwell, say not another word!" said his mother sternly.

"You had the bright idea of telling me to set the machine going as you couldn't do this yourself, but you didn't think to check that the book was actually in the library? By the Lord Harry, I must've been drunk to agree! And I was in too much of a hurry to get outside and appear at the front door when the stableboys rushed to our aid. Neither of us makes a very good plotter." Cromwell seemed to be amused by their own ineptitude. "So, Father, is my Grand Tour on or off?"

"Off!" growled his father.

"Then I'll take my horse, sell her, and head for Paris. From the news reports, I think it might be an interesting place to visit this summer. Don't expect me back any time soon, Mama. I don't think we'll be welcome here in future, do you?" Cromwell bowed over Annette's hand. "I apologize for jilting you, but if we're going to lose the Abbey, then I'm not much of a catch, am I?"

Annette patted his hand. "It was only ever the library I fancied."

With a salute to the company, Cromwell took Arachne from Deepti and led the mare away.

"Come back with my horse!" shouted Sir Charles. He turned on his audience. "Get out, all of you!" He thrust a finger under Lord Withers's nose. "And I'll see you in court!"

Flanked by two glowering sons, Lord Withers gave him a curt bow. "I look forward to it." He clicked his fingers at the nearest of his boys. "Raleigh, ride to Winchester and see that young Fitzwilliam is set free."

"Father." With a bow, Raleigh took off at a run for the stables.

"He'll need me to saddle a horse," said Luke, swinging down from Romeo. He handed the leading rein to Sir Charles. "Sir, your horse. Returned."

"Out! I never want to see you again!" bellowed Sir Charles.

Annette departed with her mother, heading back to the house. Deepti slipped away among the guests, too wise to bring any more attention to herself. Confusion reigned at the front door as Parks had to contend with scores of important people, all demanding their carriages at once.

The ballroom lawn was now relatively quiet, with only the orchestra left packing away their instruments and servants clearing the debris of hastily abandoned glasses.

"Oh, Charles, what have you done?" wailed Lady Cromwell. "Stealing your own horses!"

"And what about you?" he growled at her. "Telling our son to destroy the evidence in such a stupid fashion? We could've bought Fitzwilliam off, as I told you when you confessed what you'd done."

"That's not fair. You were the one who suggested we have him arrested!"

Sir Charles pulled on his silk cravat. "Yes, well… and all would've gone smoothly if your companion had kept out of our business!"

"You were the one who brought her here, just so you didn't have to discuss ballgowns with me!"

Jane got up from her seat on the conductor's box, deciding that Deepti had the right idea, intriguing though this conversation was.

"Where is she?" Sir Charles swung around. "You, girl! I want you gone at once! Immediately. Your things will be sent on after you, but you are not to enter my house ever again!"

"But, sir, it's almost midnight!" protested Jane.

"You should've thought of that before you meddled in our affairs. Go!" So incensed was he that he entirely forgot good manners, seizing her arm and pushing her in the direction of the gate.

Jane pulled her arm free. "I'm fetching my dog first."

"If I see that creature here in an hour, I'll shoot it on sight!"

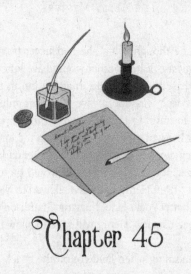

Chapter 45

Jane could tell he would very much like to turn his gun on her too, and might well do so. "Fine. We're going."

"Charles, it's night-time – she's just a girl – what will the neighbours think?" said Lady Cromwell.

"Do you really think any of them will have time to gossip about a Miss Jane Austen with everything else that has happened tonight to more important people?"

Jane could feel his gaze burning into her back as she stomped away to the stables. She would not be scared. She was an Austen. She would have Grandison with her.

In the confusion of horses and carriages, Jane could see none of her friends. Grandison found her quickly, though, and ministered comforting licks to her fingers.

"I've been having such an adventure," Jane admitted, scratching him between the ears. "And I think we're about to have another one." She took Sir Charles's threat against her dog seriously. Her hour was almost up. There was really nothing else for it. "Ready for a walk?"

Fine carriages rattled past Jane and Grandison as they retraced the road to the inn. It was pitch dark and she was scared to the bone. Jane prayed someone would offer a lift but either they didn't see her, or didn't want to be associated with the scandalous scenes they were hurrying to describe in letters and gossip to all their friends in the county.

It was lucky, Jane thought, that she had never been introduced by name to the ball guests, or her mother would have kittens.

Footsore, she arrived with Grandison at the inn in the small hours. The southbound coach was due at five in the morning. She had just enough for a seat to travel to Dean Gate, the inn nearest to Steventon, her mother having insisted on her always having the funds so she could come home in an emergency. But her mother, in her darkest forebodings, could not have imagined that her daughter would be turned out in the middle of the night. Even Henry had been allowed to wait until daylight.

"I've gone one better," said Jane, hugging Grandison as they huddled together by the coach stand. "Henry will have to allow me that."

It was ten in the morning when Jane got off the coach at Dean Gate to the bemused stares of the other passengers.

"Thank you!" she called the coachman, who had been very civil to her when he'd drawn up at the inn, and indeed expressed concern on her behalf. He had girls her age at home, he'd said.

He tapped the brim of his hat and urged the coach forward.

Jane sighed, looking up at the fingerpost. It was five miles to Steventon and she had a blister on her heel.

"Miss Jane? Good gracious: fancy meeting you here!"

Jane's heart flip-flopped between pleasure at hearing a familiar voice, and dread that it had to be – George Watson! God had a very strange sense of humour if this was the way he answered her prayers for help.

"Mr Watson." She bobbed a curtsey.

He looked about him. "Are you here alone?"

And that was quite a scandal, so Jane had to think quickly.

"I've been staying with… er… friends. The maid they sent with me fell ill at the last inn. I had to go on by myself."

"And your family isn't here to meet you?"

"No, I… er… had to leave quite suddenly due to a change in my hosts' plans." *Like fighting to keep their ancestral estate.* "My family doesn't know I'm on my way home a few days early."

"In that case, Miss Jane, might I offer you a lift?" He must've caught her momentary panicked expression. "I assure you I will take it very slowly. I've learned my lesson. I give you my word as a gentleman."

More blisters or believe in his promise?

"Thank you, Mr Watson. Grandison and I would be much obliged."

His pace could not be faulted. If anything, George drove as if heading to a funeral. Jane made note that she would have to tell Cassandra she was allowed to like him, just a little.

He drove her up to the rectory door. The crunch of wheels brought Henry, her mother, and father from the house. Cassandra hovered in the passage, still forbidden to show her broken arm to strangers, but her face revealed her delight to have her sister home. Grandison barked enthusiastically. If her mother hadn't realized he was gone, then she would now, thought Jane with resignation. Now she was in for a scolding for failing.

"Jane! Good lord, whatever brings you back home so soon?" Her mother was quickly calculating what must've happened. "You must've started your journey at first light."

No, actually in the middle of the night.

"Thank you, Mr Watson," said Jane.

"My pleasure, Miss Jane," he said. He tipped his hat to Cassandra, having spotted her lurking. That would make her sister's day.

Henry held the horses' heads while Jane stepped down from the carriage and into her father's arms.

"Oh, my dear girl, are you all right?" her father asked gruffly.

"I am now," said Jane.

Chapter 46

The family waited until George had left before interrogating her as to the events of the last few days. Henry – and even her mild-mannered father – were all for going directly to the Abbey and giving Sir Charles a drubbing for putting her through the scandal of a coach journey with no chaperone and in the middle of the night too!

"From what Jane says, Sir Charles is going to get quite a put-down from his peers for his disgraceful behaviour. Thank goodness you took Grandison with you! But we must never speak of it again," her mother declared predictably. "We need not draw attention to Jane's part in this – it will do her reputation no good and will serve no useful purpose. Jane –"

"I know, Mama: I must not mention it in my diary or my letters."

Mrs Austen hugged her younger daughter to her breast. "I'm very proud of you."

Jane cleared the lump in her throat, astounded by her mother's reaction. "Oh, Mama. I was so scared."

"That's not to say if I catch you investigating crimes again, I'll have to…" She couldn't think of a sufficiently awful threat.

"Yes, Mama?" Jane asked.

"… Forbid you from reading any more novels – for a year!"

That brought protests from everyone else, including Jane's father, who liked to read aloud to them in the evenings. "Well, maybe a month. All right: a week!"

They all agreed that was a fair punishment for an Austen.

Henry waited until their mother had gone to check on the stew for dinner and their father retired to his study to write his sermon on the evils of gambling. He tossed her the prize money.

"But I didn't catch the ghost. I think it was Sir Charles – to keep us all out of the ruins – but I can't be sure!" protested Jane.

"But you *became* the ghost – and that's even better!" Henry declared.

Cassandra agreed that she had exceeded all expectations of an Austen so Jane kept the money.

That night, as they lay together in their bed, Jane told Cassandra all the details she had omitted from the family account.

"I really liked Luke and Deepti, and I think you would too," she said.

Cassandra lay on her back, broken arm at her side. "A stableboy and a girl from India – my, you have been having an adventure."

Jane could hear the note of jealousy. "But they aren't you, Cassandra. I missed my favourite sister."

"As you pointed out, I'm your *only* sister."

"You got that letter?"

"I did. Very amusing. But next time, when you want to investigate something as exciting as an abbey ghost, take me with you, please?"

Jane tapped Cassandra on the nose. "Deal."

Life had settled back to its usual routine. Never had Jane more appreciated her father's gentle Christian faith and her mother's good works as they both went around the parish of Steventon. Compared to Sir Charles and Lady Cromwell and the way they treated their estate, hers had proved the very best kind of parents. She was grateful she'd grown up with their example rather than the one Cromwell had had in his life. As a result of this realization, Jane even carried her share of baskets without complaint, a change that surprised Cassandra.

The Hampshire newspapers, Jane was amused to see, were full of the events of the ball but her mother was relieved to see her daughter was only described as "Lady Cromwell's young companion", so enjoyed joining the gossip with the neighbours. When asked if Cassandra had gone to keep the lady company as Mrs Austen had mentioned might be a possibility, Mrs Austen had looked wide-eyed at Mrs Biggs.

"Why no," she said as the women sat sewing together in her parlour with Jane sitting demurely bedside her. "Poor Cassandra has been laid up with a fever these last weeks. That must have been quite some other girl."

And her neighbours all agreed that the Austens had had a lucky escape not to be mixed up in the disgraceful goings-on at Southmoor.

Three weeks after her return, Jane was walking through the village with Grandison, when she heard a horse behind her. Turning, she shaded her eyes against the low shafts of sunlight, making out the silhouette of a man and a boy riding pillion.

Grandison knew who it was at once. He barked excitedly and ran toward the horse with every intention, it appeared, of scaring it into bolting.

"Grandison!"

Chapter 47

Disaster was averted when a cricket ball sailed overhead, and Grandison bounded in the opposite direction.

"Miss Austen!" called Fitzwilliam.

"Hello, Jane," said Luke, from behind him.

"We are both so relieved to see you safe and well," said Fitzwilliam.

Luke slid off the horse and held the head while Fitzwilliam dismounted.

"When we heard what Sir Charles had done, we had to check you were all right in person," said Luke as Grandison dropped the ball at his feet.

"I'm quite well, thank you. My lapdog kept me company on the journey. I told you he'd be useful." Jane smiled happily at them both. Her friends had not forgotten her. "And you? How are you both?"

"Not in gaol, thanks to you, though it took a while for them to decide to release me," said Fitzwilliam.

"Deepti and Luke were as much to do with that as I."

"But you were the one who put it together. I'm in your debt."

"I must introduce you to my family – come to tea," said Jane, pointing toward the rectory.

"That would be most welcome, but may we first not catch up on your news? I want to hear everything that happened after I was taken away. That looks a pleasant spot, Miss Jane – shall we sit?" Fitzwilliam indicated a bench by the church gate.

Jane agreed with him that this was a good plan. Once her family got involved she was unlikely to be able to get a word in edgeways. When she had finished her account, she turned to Fitzwilliam.

"Now you must tell me how you both are. Are you still at the Abbey?"

Fitzwilliam shook his head. "I'm never to darken their door again, apparently, nor my father. Fortunately, Lord Withers has taken upon himself to find employment for my father and he is paying for me to return to university. He says he might be in need of a good lawyer if he cannot reach a gentleman's agreement with Sir Charles to settle the matter of the inheritance."

"What kind of agreement?"

"Lord Withers has a daughter still in the schoolroom. There's talk she might be betrothed to Cromwell when he gets back from the continent – though I'm not sure when that will be. Did you hear about the Bastille?"

Jane shook her head. Word travelled slowly to this part of Hampshire.

"The Parisians have pulled down their most infamous prison. There's talk of revolution. Cromwell will be delighted."

"And when exactly did he arrive in Paris?" asked Jane archly.

Fitzwilliam laughed.

"And what about the low trick of blaming you for everything?" asked Jane. "Don't tell me that no one is to be punished for that?"

Luke snorted. "It was a joke, wasn't it?"

"Sir Charles claims it was all a play for the guests' entertainment at a gothic-themed ball – illuminated ruins, wild riders, even an appearance by the Mad Monk."

"And does anyone actually believe that?"

"By the time the story is passed around the salons of London, he'll have some crediting his tale, maybe enough to salvage his respectability. As it is, I imagine he and Lady Cromwell will lie low for a while, until the talk dies down."

"I hope he has to untangle her silks," said Jane stoutly.

"You are a cruel girl," said Fitzwilliam, "though I agree that is a punishment worse than imprisonment in Winchester lock-up."

"What about you, Luke? What are you going to do?" asked Jane.

"I'm sticking with Sir here. He needs someone with a bit of sense to keep him out of gaol," said Luke.

Fitzwilliam rubbed his knuckles on the boy's scalp. "I'm taking this know-it-all to Oxford with me. And I'll make sure he gets to see all the mechanical exhibitions and meet as many engineers as I can find."

That sounded like it would suit them both perfectly.

"And Deepti?"

"Sir Charles won't give up his Hindoo cook so has chosen to ignore her part in the sudden arrival of the horses at the ball. But the good news there is that they have sent for the rest of their family and hope they will arrive by the end of the year."

"But I might never see her again if she stays at Southmoor!" Jane knew she would not be allowed within ten miles of the Abbey if Sir Charles had his way.

"There is always letter-writing," said Fitzwilliam.

"She asked that you write to her like you did to your sister when you were at the Abbey," said Luke.

Wait a moment... "How does she know I wrote to my sister?"

"She said she saw your notes on the desk when she went into your room on that first day. Grandison was whining, so she let him out."

"So it was her!"

"She thought you wouldn't mind her going in – better than coming back to a puddle in your room. She never had a chance to tell you. Anyway, she said she would like to correspond, as she doesn't want to lose one of the few friends she has in England."

That made Jane feel better. "Then I will. Shall we go in for tea? My family has heard so much about you that they won't forgive me for letting you get away."

"Will there be cake as well as Austen outrageousness?" asked Luke.

"Probably, if Henry has left us any."

"And novel-reading, full of fantastical events like ghosts and wicked barons?" asked Fitzwilliam.

"Undoubtedly."

"Then lead on. That sounds just the tea party for us."

Jane, Fitzwilliam, and Luke walked toward the rectory. She could see her mother already at the door, shading her eyes to see who was coming to call. The order to put the kettle on would have been given. Jane was already composing her letter to Deepti in her mind.

To be ruled by the letter "D", she decided, in honour of her friend's name. A little note before a longer one, to check all was well.

A Deeply Felt Letter

Dearest Deepti,

Distance doesn't dull desolation endured by direct departure before dawn from despotic deceiver's demesne. Delightfully, though, dog delivered me dependably to dwelling place without deviation. Dire deeds described to distressed Daddy and his dear ones. My detective doings declared deceased (but don't you depend on it!).

Do dictate your deeds since date of my dismissal to declare all decent with dad and daughter.

Dispatched by yr devoted damsel,

Jane